When the World Wounds

by Kiini Ibura Salaam

THIRD MAN BOOKS
NASHVILLE, TENNESSEE

Also by Kiini Ibura Salaam:

FICTION
Ancient, Ancient (Aqueduct Press 2012)

NONFICTION
On the Psychology of Writing (Brilliant Editions 2012)
On the Struggle to Self-Promote (Brilliant Editions 2013)
On the Push to Produce Work (Brilliant Editions 2014)

WHEN THE WORLD WOUNDS

KIINI IBURA SALAAM

More about Kiini Ibura Salaam:

thirdmanbooks.com/whentheworldwounds
password: volcanowoman

Printed in Nashville, Tennessee

Library of Congress Control Number: 2016954167

FIRST EDITION
Design by Ryon Nishimori
Cover Illustration by Rachel Briggs

ISBN   978-0-9913361-5-9

To all the wild and wise ones who are helping me raise my daughter
so that when the world wounds she knows how to react, adapt and snapback.

CONTENTS

THE MALADY OF NEED

He would have looked at you like he knew all your truths. You would have wanted to unearth the secrets you saw buried in his eyes. You'd have caught his glance and your dick would have gone stiff. You would have imagined him licking your chest, your ankles, his own perfect lips.

You would have traded a week's worth of protein to get your work detail changed, to shatter the barriers between you, to ride with him only a breath away. Had you any gods you would have thanked them for the nutters who were always trying to escape. Even as your shackled hands were pulled tight over your head, you would have felt love for lockdown. When the lights cut, you would have eased yourself forward, slipping around the others, easing your tether forward as you moved into his orbit.

He would have whipped around when you stood behind him, then shushed you when you tried to explain. He would have brushed against you and you would have swayed with him, surprised to feel the tug of want stirring in your loins. When the shuttle lights blinked back on, he would have sighed before forcing blankness back into his face. You would have been left with tremors, tiny spasms whispering your need.

You would have begun to starve yourself. You would go without to nourish him. You would bring him only the best of your rations—long grasshoppers roasted crunchy, thick red caterpillars, the ones with the sweet meat. It would be the only time you would have been able to touch him—in the few seconds after your hands had been released from the shackles. You would have smiled as he slipped your food into his zip suit. It would have pleased you to think of objects you had handled resting against his skin.

He would have been thick. With pounds of flesh that could cushion all your hates and angers. You would have lost hours slack-jawed, staring into space, fantasizing about the press of his flesh.

He would have started to make demands. He would have wanted you to mark yourself, to draw blood. He would have wanted to see the scabs, the thin lines that prove how much you want him. You would have begun to enjoy it. It would have felt electric to think of him as you severed your skin. As you bled, you would have imagined him, alone in his bunk, his fingers doing the work your dick had been dying to do.

Your thoughts of him would have become incessant. You would have been thinking about him when they came for you in the night. You would have been desperate to cling to your thoughts of him as they shackled you to the rack. You would have strained to remember the contours of his mouth as they plunged the tubes into your back. You would have tried to re-create his scent as the machine began to whir. They would have begun to drain your blood, as you were imagining yourself slipping inside him. Then the pain would have overwhelmed you. You would have gone slack as everything around you melted away.

He would have known. As soon as he had seen you, he would have known that they had come for you. You would have wanted to stare at him, to drink in the vision of him to feed your sanity, but you would not have been able to bear it. You would have lowered your head so he could not see the mania in your eyes.

You would not have known how he did it, but you would have known that he had found a way to force the shuttle to screech to a stop. As the shackles went slack and the voices of the others rose around you, he would have come. He would have freed your wrists and touched his tongue to yours. You would have fought it. You would have tried to remember where you were. But he would not have relented.

He would have dragged your buried sobs to the surface. You would have lost yourself under the press of his lips. He would have made visions flash in your mind. Touching him, you would have remembered what the sky looked like, the taste of fresh fruit, the feel of water on your skin.

You would have wanted to stop. You would not have wanted to be this naked, this disarmed. You would have lost yourself in the slickness of his body, in the work, in the friction. The itch of the compound would have dissipated against your will. The burn of the electric wristbands would have faded. You would have straddled him and pummeled him with frantic thrusts. As if you wanted to devour him. As if you wanted to re-create him, then spit him out reborn.

When the shuttle jerked back into motion, you would not have been able to look at him. Slipping your wrists back into the shackles felt like insanity, like suicide. As you worked, his scent would have gnawed at your nostrils. You would have felt as if his dark waters were rising over your body, as if you were drowning in him.

In the morning, you will erase him from existence. You will let the day's drudgery make a meal of your heart. You will withdraw. You will lock away all softness, all surrender. When the malady comes, you will clench the corners of your lips. You will go tense as it straddles your shoulders and chokes you with your own need. You will roll over and stroke your hardness. You will come in silence, consumed by dread.

THE PULL OF THE WING

WaLiLa felt wind pressing against her face. Her body swooped downward and she was surprised to find herself floating on invisible currents. Delight thrummed through her as she marveled at the sensation of shooting through air, bouncing on magical winds that kept her aloft.

There was a loud boom and the winds dissolved. Everything around her trembled and her body was suddenly heavy. Instead of stretched out in ecstatic flight, her body was cramped and curled into itself. When she tried to flex her limbs, her sleeping shroud pressed against her skin, hemming her in. WaLiLa shifted her shoulders. She did need to touch her back to know that the expanse of her upper back was empty.

She began to wriggle, furiously pushing at the layers of the sleeping shroud until she had opened a slit she could peek through. The room was still and the others—hanging in neat rows all around her—were silent in sleep. She watched their shrouded forms swaying slightly, the thrill of flying still fluttering in her chest. Once the reality of her wingless existence was firmly settled into her skin, she grasped the edges of her shroud and retreated back into darkness.

Before sleep returned, WaLiLa felt MalKai stir next to her. She peeked her head out again and watched his arms shifting through the translucent folds of his shroud. She wondered if he was dreaming of flying, if—in his fidgeting—he was trying to stretch out his arms as if they were giant wings he could spread wide. When his feeling hands were pressed overhead and his middle arms were wound tightly around his torso, he stopped squirming and settled back into stillness.

When a fierce itch flared up between WaLiLa's shoulder blades, she decided chasing sleep was useless. She placed her six palms together, wriggled them through the opening of the shroud, and pushed her arms outward, coaxing the shroud away from her body. Flexing her feet and separating her ankles, she cut the filaments that kept her suspended from the ceiling. Stretching her feeling hands out overhead, she spread her middle arms wide as she tumbled to the floor. The fall to the floor was the closest she had ever come to flight. On her way down, she kicked out in MalKai's direction and jammed her foot into his side before landing on the floor.

WaLiLa crouched low on the floor until MalKai jerked awake. When she was sure he had seen her, she drifted away to search the rows of sleeping trainees for RaLinWa. That the other trainees could sleep this way—deeply all through day dark—disgusted her. They had spent all their young lives sleeping in random spurts, with no one to monitor when they woke. Here in the training compound, everything was different. Life had an order and a routine. That the other trainees had adjusted so easily to the compound's rigid rules proved to WaLiLa that they were blind followers who would accept being left wingless after the training if the Elders didn't choose them to receive wings. WaLiLa didn't plan to leave the compound without a taste of flight.

WaLiLa finally found RaLinWa in the rear, hanging near the curved wall of the sleeping chamber. When WaLiLa nudged her, RaLinWa slowly swung back and forth but didn't stir. The trainee in the next shroud shifted, grazing WaLiLa as he pushed against his shroud, working to create an opening the layers. The trainee peeked out and WaLiLa turned her back. He wriggled his feeling hands out of the shroud and tapped her on the shoulder.

What are you doing? he asked with quick fluttering motions. WaLiLa arced her feeling palms flat overhead and flicked her four lower hands backward, dismissing any conversation. She shuttered the row of lenses across the back of her skull just to make it clear to LorSenKiPe that she had nothing to say to him.

WaLiLa nudged RaLinWa a second time and again, RaLinWa did not rouse. LorSenKiPe stretched his arm out of his shroud, reached past WaLiLa, and scratched up RaLinWa's side. RaLinWa shivered, then woke with a startled jerk.

You're welcome, LorSenKiPe motioned over WaLiLa's shoulder.

WaLiLa ignored him, focusing instead on flipping open the lenses in the back of her head and checking that no one else was awake. She saw MalKai creeping toward her, careful not to jostle the sleeping trainees around him. When he reached WaLiLa, he vibrated his lower fingers in front of his knees and circled the longest fingers on his feeling hands in the air.

Why are we awake? I thought we were doing searches every other cycle.

WaLiLa reached back and tapped her shoulder blades with her feeling hands while pressing her middle hands against her head. She ended by splaying the fingers on four of her hands.

The dream. Didn't you have it?

Yes, and you interrupted it.

WaLiLa glanced at RaLinWa who had been stirring, but was now slumping back into sleep. She pressed her middle hands against her head again and trembled her feeling hands, palms down. *You think RaLinWa's having it now?*

I wish I was having it now, MalKai motioned sarcastically.

WaLiLa reached out to yank at RaLinWa's sleeping shroud, but MalKai smacked her arm.

Don't do that. He curved his back, slumping his shoulders, and flipped all six hands up and down, one after the other. *You know you hate it if someone opens your shroud while you're sleeping.*

I wasn't going to take her shroud off, crawler. I was just trying to wake her up.

In the midst of their argument, the sleeping chamber trembled. They fell into each other, then quickly regained their footing as the cocooned trainees hanging on both sides of them swayed with the chamber's vibrations.

Do you think the compound is going to collapse? LorSenKiPe motioned, emerging from his shroud again, but WaLiLa and MalKai huddled together and ignored him. He motioned a few obscene gestures at their backs.

It's coming from the chamber, she motioned. *The wings are calling us.*

You don't know that, MalKai replied.

LorSenKiPe pushed his shroud off his shoulders. *What chamber?* he motioned while still hanging upside down.

Nothing, WaLiLa motioned dryly. *Go back to sleep, Lor.*

LorSenKiPe shivered in annoyance and replaced his shroud. WaLiLa and MalKai edged around RaLinWa to continue their conversation in privacy.

Check the plan, she motioned.

You want to try it now? MalKai motioned wildly.

WaLiLa grabbed his hands and jerked her head toward LorSenKiPe.

We don't know what's in there, he motioned more calmly.

Wings! WaLiLa motioned. *Wings are in there. Check the plan.*

WaLiLa closed her eyes and went still. After a few wingbeats, she peeked at MalKai. His eyes were closed and his body was still. She closed her eyes again and started by attempting the impossible—scanning the inside of the mysterious chamber at the heart of the training compound. She was not surprised when that failed—again. Without a pause, she switched her focus to checking the plan. She ran every detail of their plan through her message- center to research the risks and possibilities associated with breaking into the chamber. Her message-center pulsed, busily calculating the risk of getting caught (two slivers less than three-fourths moon) and analyzing the extent of punishment should they get caught (any trainee caught breaking rules of trespass was neutralized, removed from the assignment roster, and kept inert until their cohort's missions had ended).

When she opened her eyes, MalKai was staring at her.

Two slivers less than three-fourths moon, they motioned simultaneously.

It's the lowest it's ever been, WaLiLa motioned.

MalKai crossed his arms. *We made a pact, remember. No more than a half moon of risk.*

That was before the reprimand!

MalKai spread the fingers on his feeling hands. *I know.*

We won't be getting wings now, not unless someone fails their mission.

What about RaWa?

Behind them, RaLinWa's shroud unwound and slipped to the floor.

RaWa is awake now, thanks to you two clumsy crawlers. What's a half a moon of risk? she motioned before flipping herself horizontal and arcing to the floor.

The plan, WaLiLa motioned. *The risk went down to two slivers less than three-fourths. It's time. You joining?*

RaLinWa rippled her fingers then closed her hands into fists.

So you two got caught and now you want me to risk losing out on a mission to help you get wings anyway.

Sounds right, MalKai motioned, repeatedly tapping his   elbows with two fingers.

There was a pause. RaLinWa swayed back and forth as she did when she was thinking. Then she whirled her hands overhead.

Really? WaLiLa motioned, leaping up and down with excitement.

Can't have you two discovering the secrets of the chamber without me, she motioned.

The three of them slapped hands, then turned in unison to weave their way past the hanging bodies of their sleeping cohort. The moment they slipped out of the sleeping chamber, they fell into formation, following one behind the other to slide through space as one unit. When they had advanced for one hundred wingbeats, they paused. With the fluidity of seasons of practice honed during frequent childhood mischief, they closed their eyes in unison. They were still as they connected to the fine lines of energy that crisscrossed through the dirt-packed walls of the training compound. WaLiLa and MalKai had been reprimanded for a much smaller infraction than interfering with the Elder's monitoring systems. They had been caught in an area of the compound they had not been given permission to access. RaLinWa would say that it was her superior sneaking stills that had protected her from getting caught. WaLiLa would say that RaLinWa was just lucky.

As trainees, WaLiLa, MalKai, and RaLinWa should not have been able to access the Elders' systems, but they had long since discovered that when the three of them joined forces, they could thwart many obstacles. In the coolness of the tunnel outside the sleeping chamber, the three friends worked together to follow the energy lines to the Elders' data collection hub. There they scoured the output lines for any data related to their whereabouts. When they located the record of their presence in the hallways outside the sleeping chamber, they were startled to find that the Elders' system had tracked not three blips of energy moving through the tunnels of the training compound, but four. According to the data, the fourth energy was following just behind RaLinWa. The three friends spun around to see LorSenKiPe standing right behind RaLinWa, eyes wide with fright.

Just as quickly, they turned forward again and took a few wingbeats of deep stillness to suppress their alarm. Manipulating the data the Elders used to monitor the training compound required focus and precision. In their early forays of exploring the complex system that threaded through the network of buried hallways and chambers, they had learned that influencing the system opened a two-way portal. Once joined to the monitoring system, any spike in emotion would trigger alerts, dispatching Elders to the site in question, aborting their adventure before it began.

Without discussion, they pressed on, ignoring LorSenKiPe so they could maintain their balancing act of stealth and progress. They were cautious and thorough as they moved through the winding hallways of the training compound, stopping every so often to access the Elder's records, ferreting out the records of their and LorSenKiPe's presence and destroying them before they could be shot out into the Elders' consciousness from the system's message center.

When they were nearing their destination, the walls began to emit a faint blue glow, and the space on their upper backs, between their shoulders began to itch. As they drifted closer and closer to the heart of the compound, they had to work harder to suppress their emotions. The itching had preceded the dreams. At first the itching was just a strange sensation they noticed they were the only trainees to suffer from. But when they stumbled into the area of the compound that was flooded with blue light, a fever washed over them and their dreams were overtaken by sensations of flight.

The fever transformed them, feeding them with a frenzied need to experience flight. They told themselves they wouldn't jeopardize their missions as they started to plot. Their forays through the compound eased the intolerableness of being sequestered underground in the training compound. Their adventures were thrilling as they practiced tapping into the Elders' system and manipulating insignificant details. They were positively giddy when they discovered the chamber where the blue glow was the strongest. When they stood outside that chamber, the itch between their shoulders exploded into a burning sensation. They collectively attempted to get a view of what was inside, but their vision centers were too weak and they were unable to peer into the chamber.

Even though they were careful enough to split up after their searches, their failure to see inside the chamber dulled their vigilance and two of them were caught. Undaunted by the sanction, they switched tactics and decided to spy on the chamber rather than attempt to see inside. They discovered that the chamber could be unsealed by Elder speak. They used the Elders' monitoring system to copy the exact sequence of motions the Elders used to open the chamber. From then on, the danger was not getting caught in the wrong part of the compound, it was memorizing the Elder speak without getting caught.

Once they had succeeded at replicating the movements with fluidity and precision, they had to decide whether or not to enter the chamber. Rather than decide, they waited, each of them taking turns spurring the plan forward and urging caution. As they waited, they debated the question of the wings.

Do you think the wings will turn us into Elders? MalKai had asked.

WaLiLa flicked the fingers of all six hands open. *If they did, I would rip them right off.*

You're going to have to be an Elder one day, RaLinWa motioned. *You can't stop the cycles.*

I won't ever live like them. She swiveled around, the twist of her hip emphasizing her seriousness.

The three friends went still as they imagined themselves back in the fields, dwarfed by rows of tall, thick-stemmed dew catchers, swarms of Elders darkening the sky as they flew across the dome overhead.

Will we even recognize each other when we become Elders? MalKai asked.

They all look the same, WaLiLa motioned, imagining the Elders ensconced in the sterile environment of the dome—flying, perching, mating. Life in the fields was full of dew catchers, animals, and burrows, whereas the Elders' side of the dome seemed to be a vast open space of nothingness. No plants, no dust, no tunnels. WaLiLa and her friends found the dome frightening.

I thought the Elders were travelers. Seems like they never leave that dome.

RaLinWa fluttered one of her feeling hands overhead. *One day you two crawlers will learn, there's more going on than what you can see.*

I hope so, because they look boring, like lazy lumps, waiting around for us to bring them nectar, MalKai motioned.

The nectar takes them places, and one day we will travel with it too, RaLinWa motioned.

The nectar? WaLiLa motioned. *Is it like pollen?*

Do you two pay attention to anything?!? RaLinWa asked, pressing her feeling hands to her face in exaggerated exhaustion while her middle arms gesticulated wildly. *The Elders keep life going. Without them we would have no food, no....*

I thought the Grand-Elders kept everything going, WaLiLa motioned.

At the mention of the Grand-Elders, RaLinWa went still. After a few wingbeats, she motioned suddenly. *Forget about the Grand-Elders, we'll never find out what they do. All you need to know is that wings don't turn you into Elders. Missions do.*

I thought missions gave you wings, WaLiLa motioned.

MalKai began to float his arms up in conversation before he had fully processed his thoughts. *What if...? What if...taking these wings changes everything and they don't let us become Elders?*

WaLiLa made a flat plane with her hand and flipped it from her mouth to her eyes. *I think we ruined that already. Besides, can you imagine it? Wings without being Elders?!? It would be worth it.*

Then they had gone still, imagining the possibility of completely altering the cycles of their future. Yet, even as they had stared at each other, letting the enormity of what they contemplated doing wash over them, not one of them questioned if they would continue. Small rebellions had cemented their childhood, each embracing recklessness for a different reason. RaLinWa was a mystic on a spiritual path to unravel life's mysteries at whatever cost. MalKai was a staunch believer in a personal freedom—even at his most obedient, he reserved the right to tweak the rules to his liking. WaLiLa was a disrupter by nature. Driven by a need to poke at things and reveal their underbelly in order to quell the agitation that surfaced in her whenever she was faced with a mystery or a puzzle. No matter how grave, none of them hesitated to pay the price for their adventures, and their trust was exclusive to each other. Any time they had tried to bring others into their confidence, they found their plans ruined, so when they finally reached the chamber, the first thing the three of them did was whip around to confront LorSenKipe.

What are we doing here? LorSenKiPe motioned before they could express their anger.

No, WaLiLa motioned. *What are* you *doing here?* She shoved LorSenKiPe in the chest.

I... LorSenKiPe started to explain, then stopped.

What are we going to do now? WaLiLa motioned, turning away from him with disgust.

We can't send him back alone, motioned MalKai. *We'll get caught.*

I'm not leaving without going in, WaLiLa argued.

The three friends paused abruptly and closed their eyes. In the stillness, they scanned the system, and dissolved the record of their presence, before resuming the conversation.

We're not responsible for him, WaLiLa motioned.

Yes, we are, RaLinWa replied.

He'll ruin everything, MalKai motioned.

Well, he's here now and we made it to the chamber, RaLinWa interrupted. *The only solution is we tell him and move forward with the plan.*

Before anyone replied, the three of them closed their eyes and went still. When they had erased the proof of their presence along with LorSenKiPe's, WaLiLa motioned, *We don't have time for this. You want to tell him? You do it. Mal and I will open the chamber.* She turned to LorSenKiPe. *You should not have come.*

LorSenKiPe started to motion his reply, but WaLiLa stopped him. *YOU SHOULD NOT HAVE COME!*

She stepped away from LorSenKiPe and stood in front of the entrance to the chamber. She clasped her hands and looked at MalKai. He joined her at the entrance and clasped his hands around hers. Then they began. At the outset, when they were learning this sequence, the motions had felt awkward. None of the movements were in their regular language—this was Elder-speak, marked by elongations and sustained pauses that required WaLiLa's full attention. As WaLiLa and MalKai struggled through the motions, RaLinWa was standing not even a wingspan away, motioning wildly as she explained the plan to LorSenKipe. Out of the corner of her eye, WaLiLa saw LorSenKiPe's hands shoot out and his arms flap in shock. As her attention strayed, she faltered. She quickened her motions to catch up, but it was too late. She finished the last steps of the sequence half a wingbeat after MalKai.

The dance complete, WaLiLa and MalKai stood in front of the chamber with their hands at their sides. They waited for the entrance to open, but nothing happened.

You were off, MalKai motioned.

I know. It's Lor's fault.

Don't blame Lor, RaLinWa motioned. *Focus, or we'll have to go back with nothing.*

WaLiLa turned to face MalKai. She took a few breaths and clasped her hands. MalKai clasped his hands around hers and they began again. WaLiLa pushed away her jitters and willed herself to focus only on the shapes MalKai made with his body. Through sheer force, she timed each of her movements in perfect synchronicity with MalKai's. She knew they had succeeded when the chamber started to react before they had even finished the dance. As they entered the last sequence, the chamber's sealed entrance peeled back one layer, then two. Then, in concert with the last steps of the dance, the final layer sealing the chamber's entrance split down the middle and peeled away. The four of them were so stunned that for a few wingbeats they stayed frozen in place. Then WaLiLa grasped MalKai's hand, MalKai grabbed RaLinWa, and RaLinWa dragged LorSenKipe along with them as they stumbled into the chamber.

The moment all four trainees had crossed the entranceway, the chamber sealed itself shut behind them. As they stood huddled near the entranceway, a wet chill engulfed them. Then a rumbling rolled through the chamber, causing an intense vibration that almost knocked them off their feet. They gripped each other, furtively looking around the chamber. With the exception of a large round platform in the center, the space was empty.

No wings! MalKai motioned.

No one responded. They were too captivated by two shrouded forms lying on the platform in the center of the chamber. A bright blue light shone on the platform, illuminating the forms and leaving the rest of the chamber cloaked in heavy shadows. Staring at the forms, all they could see was the stiff and tattered outer wrapping of shrouds that looked horribly ancient and papery thin.

LorSenKiPe broke the stillness with trembling arms. *I thought we were here for wings. What is that?*

RaLinWa shushed him with a savage swipe of her arm.

We need to leave now! she motioned to the other two.

Before either WaLiLa or MalKai could answer, there was a soft rustling overhead. They slowly looked up. In the dimness of the chamber, they could just make out the forms of large fuzzy wings lying flat across the length of the ceiling. The burning sensation between their shoulders felt as if it were boring through their skin. WaLiLa felt herself yanked erect, as if her cells were straining upward. A profound longing swooped through her, pushing the chamber away from her consciousness. She was lost in the contours of the wings when she felt MalKai jab her hard in her side. She snapped back into awareness and shot MalKai a sharp look.

Grand-Elders?!?! LorSenKiPe was motioning.

Grand-Elders? WaLiLa repeated. *Here?*

Why are they lying there? Why aren't they hanging? Are they dead? LorSenKiPe motioned, his terror causing him to blur and stutter his motions.

We are done here, MalKai motioned.

Why? You think they'll stop us from taking the wings? WaLiLa motioned back.

RaLinWa smacked WaLiLa's arm. *Forget the wings. These are Grand-Elders. We can't do anything they don't command.*

What are they going to do to us? LorSenKiPe motioned.

We don't have time to discuss this, MalKai motioned. *We should go now.*

LorSenKiPe was the first to turn away.

What's the dance to get out? he motioned.

There was an awkward wing beat of stillness. The three friends looked at each other, then motioned simultaneously, *We didn't practice that.*

LorSenKiPe slapped his feeling palms against his middle palms in an expression of disgust.

They began to argue, furiously flailing their arms. The explosion of blame slowly began to wane as they felt shallow, slippery breaths stretching outward from the unmoving forms and winnowing toward them to curl around their bodies in tightening tendrils.

A blast of sound exploded inside each of them, causing them to jerk in horror, then freeze.

You all felt that? WaLiLa motioned.

Yes, they all responded with a quick flick of their elbows.

When they were still, they could feel the lick of breath as an unseen force probed them, pushing at their limbs and sipping at their skin. The sound blast rumbled through them again, this time collecting into a sharp pressure at the crown of each of their heads. The pressure unfurled as a pair of disembodied arms took shape in their minds, flying into body speak as soon as the images were complete.

Be still! the disembodied limbs commanded.

The four trainees focused the lenses on the back of their heads on the platform in the center of the chamber. Nothing had changed. The two forms lay there on the platform unmoved, just as cocooned and inert as when the trainees had arrived. The snaking breaths grew stronger, seeping outward from the mysterious forms with more terrifying force and volume. WaLiLa, MalKai, RaLinWa, and LorSenKiPe were perfectly still as the sound rustled around them, filling their ears with layered, raspy vibrations that quickened to mimic the fluttering of a multitude of moth wings.

Another blast of sound tore through their stunned stillness.

Approach!

With an uncharacteristic panic, RaLinWa darted forward. She stopped a few wingspans away from the platform and sank to the floor, lifting and dropping her shoulders in a hasty show of respect. She forced her face to fall into a calm façade, as she slowly rose from the floor. With as few motions as possible, she gestured each of their names, explaining that they were nothing more than curious trainees hoping to get a glance at the wings. With the most formal and graceful movements she could muster, she expressed their most sincere apologies for disturbing the Grand-Elders. She finished by motioning a shaky, but eloquent petition for the Grand-Elders' permission to leave the chamber.

When RaLinWa was still, a sloppy slurping sound filled the chamber. The sound engulfed the four trainees in a disorienting, chaotic jumble of noise that left them reeling. In the melee of sound, the disembodied arms in the trainees' minds started to flutter rapidly. At first, it seemed as if the arms were bombarding them with questions, but WaLiLa quickly realized the motions were not inquiries, they were a barrage of commands that bypassed the trainees' young message centers and went straight into their being centers. They were powerless to move as a many-legged energy crawled through them, rifling through their stored memories and poking at their histories of sensations.

In the midst of the sonic chaos, flashes of understanding broke through the confusion. There was a distinct tugging sensation and a wet pressure that made it feel as if the Grand-Elders were consuming them. Suddenly, the chamber contracted. The floor trembled, then everything went still again. In the quiet, the four trainees moved their limbs cautiously. During that brief pause, MalKai motioned, *We're never getting out of here.*

Without responding to MalKai, LorSenKiPe stepped forward. Separating himself from WaLiLa, MalKai and RaLinWa, he began to motion frantically, passionately pleading his innocence. He begged the Grand-Elders' forgiveness, insisting that he had no hand in the plan that had resulted in them invading this sanctuary. As he motioned, the icy chill in the chamber deepened. Then, before he could finish, the chamber's walls and floor heaved with a mighty pulse and he was propelled into the air. The others scrambled backward. As LorSenKiPe dangled overhead, they lined up in front of the chamber's entrance. In sheer desperation, they started doing the dance they had used to enter the room. They feverishly threw themselves into the escape attempt, but just like LorSenKiPe, they were yanked upward, one by one. Their bodies hovered close to the ceiling, their eyes darting around in complete panic as some unseen force held them suspended in air. They were beset upon by contradictory sensations. The wings—just a few breaths overhead—vibrated with an intoxicating humming. From below, the terrifying tugging of the Grand-Elders had begun to snack on them again.

Without warning, their bodies went slack and their heads lolled to one side. A fetid rotting odor overwhelmed their senses. What little power they retained was dedicated to gasping for air. Scenes of their lives flashed through their consciousness, each memory accompanied by a sharp slurping sound. They were rocked by disorientation on top of disorientation as time and space collapsed onto itself. Their physical proximity to each other in the chamber overlapped with visceral memories of the four of them together in the past. The Grand-Elders seemed to take no notice of the destabilizing impact of the juxtaposition of reality and memory. They went on, ambling through the trainees' brief but succulent history, sipping at some memories and gobbling at others.

Tumbling through the contradictions at the speed of a wingbeat, WaLiLa was gagging on the Grand-Elders' odor of rot in one moment. In the next, she had left the chamber behind. There were no greedy breaths or horrifying orders. There was just the delicious tingling of being high on pollen. She could see MalKai was standing next to her with unfocused eyes and a dreamy smile on his face. The sickening smell and the unyielding chamber—it all disappeared, and she found herself standing in the shelter of two neat rows of tall, thick-stemmed dew catchers.

I told you. Didn't I tell you? MalKai motioned.

This isn't really happening, WaLiLa wanted to motion back, but she was firmly in the memory. Her attempts at communication were unfocused, impaired by the incredible sensation of pollen coursing through her body. Awareness afforded her no control. She was aware and impotent—helpless to stop the memory from unfurling and taking over the moment. Immobilized next to her, the other trainees were struggling through the same confusing jumble of memory and reality. In MalKai's memories, LorSenKiPe was storming up to them, lower hands stretched outwards, middle hands clasped at his chest, and his feeling hands chopping through the air, demanding that they get to work. MalKai and WaLiLa were momentarily twinned in both memory and reality. In the chamber, they felt the press of each other's limp limbs. In the memory, they collapsed against each other, laughing as they flapped their hands, lightly touching fingers.

In LorSenKiPe's memory, he was lamenting his work pod placement, gesturing to no one in particular, *Why did they put me in this work pod with these crawlers?* And RaLinWa was working to keep the peace between them all.

The disembodied arms flicked their hands and all the memories cleared. For a few wingbeats, the four trainees were only aware of the Grand-Elders' breath brushing against them. They felt their bodies bobbing softly as if the entire chamber was filled with bouncing currents of air.

They're laughing, RaLinWa found the fortitude to motion, her face filled with wonder.

The disembodied arms reappeared in their minds with a blast of sound.

Amplify, the arms motioned.

At that command, the trainees' bodies went flying toward each other, the crowns of their heads skimming the wings as they slammed into each other. Their disorientation deepened as the barriers between each of them slowly melted away. When their memories took over, the four of them were standing, facing each other in the fields, the translucent petals of the dew catchers spreading across the sky overhead.

Can we get to work? The other pods are halfway done by now, RaLinWa was motioning.

For a few wingbeats no one moved. It was as if they were as confused in memory as they were in the Grand-Elders' chamber. WaLiLa was startled to feel LorSenKiPe's impatience explode inside her as if it were her own emotion. Were they all, she wondered, fluttering between each other's experiences? But then she flicked her top two wrists, there was a pulse in the memory, and they all jerked into action. WaLiLa watched herself wander over to the nearest dew catcher. She stood there, staring at the thick dew catcher stalk as if it were a foreign object. When the others didn't join her, she turned back to see LorSenKiPe squatting in the dust.

Tube's stuck, he motioned.

WaLiLa flicked her hand outward in an obscene gesture and stalked over to LorSenKiPe, completely overtaken by the memory. She reached down, grabbed the tube, and yanked it. It stretched forward, limp and pale.

You're just weak.

As soon as the insult had left her fingers, a flutter of confusing sensations exploded. The chamber tottered back into her consciousness as she felt her body bobbing again. Simultaneously, she was engulfed by a sadness that she knew to be LorSenKiPe's.

RaLinWa broke through the moment, standing between WaLiLa and LorSenKiPe. When RaLinWa nudged the tube with her foot, WaLiLa felt a solid peacefulness she had never experienced in her life. *You see this?* RaLinWa motioned. The sallow yellow of the tube was far from the deep rust it would become once full. *We don't have time for your bickering.*

Climb, the disembodied arms motioned.

As they hustled over to the base of the nearest dew catcher, WaLiLa marveled at how different it felt to root down in each of their bodies. When MalKai planted his feet in the dust, it was time to work. MalKai tensed and LorSenKiPe scrambled up MalKai's back to stand on his shoulders. As LorSenKiPe tensed, RaLinWa climbed up both MalKai and LorSenKiPe, holding tight to the dew catcher's stalk. Once the pod had solidified the tower, WaLiLa wrapped the tube around the lower part of one of her middle arms and climbed up her pod mates. During the cycles upon cycles they had spent scrambling over each other, rotating positions as they ascended the dew catchers, they had never marveled at the miracle of their collaboration. Now, under the influence of the Grand-Elders, an awe suffused their memories.

At the top, WaLiLa paused to look around. From up high, she could see the entire fields spread around her. She could hear the delighted rustle of the Grand-Elders' breath as she stared across the expanse of dew catchers. Suddenly she felt a burst of delight blossom inside her. It spread through her limbs, overwhelming her with an intensity unmatched by any pollen high. RaLinWa shrugged beneath her feet, rousing her into action. Bracing herself for the stench of the nectar, she grasped the dew catcher's petals and unwrapped the collection tube with her feeling hands. She leaned forward into the bowl of the dew catcher's petals and guided the tube down into the pool of nectar at the bottom. The tube pulsed and slinked forward to plunge into the nectar's sticky depths.

As the dew catcher began to buck back and forth under the suction of the tube, the field of dew catchers started to spiral around her. The thrum of nectar seemed deafening. She threw two of her hands over the membranes that passed sound into her body and collapsed into herself—aware only of the assault of sound.

RaLinWa appeared in WaLiLa's consciousness, motioning urgently. *Disconnect the tube. Disconnect the tube.*

WaLiLa forced her limbs into action. The second she tugged the tube away from the dew catcher, the memory dissolved with a pop and they were back in the chamber.

Before WaLiLa could see anything around her, she knew something in the chamber had changed. The chill had dissipated and she felt blasts of warm air radiating upward from below. She jerked her head around and saw that MalKai, RaLinWa, and LorSenKiPe were still next to her, hovering helplessly in the air. They were all buffeted about by cold currents whipping past them as spears of warm air shot upward from below. Gradually, the Grand-Elders' cold hold on the trainees waned. As their limbs were immersed in warm air, they were released from their paralysis.

The instant they could move, they grabbed hold of each other. Then instinct took them in different directions. WaLiLa reached upward toward the wings. MalKai extended two of his arms toward the nearest wall. RaLinWa dipped forward as if attempting to dive down to the floor. LorSenKiPe strained in the opposite direction as if trying to drag them all toward the entrance. When WaLiLa's fingers made contact with the wings, they arced away, shifting out of reach and clearing access to the ceiling.

Dig, MalKai motioned and stretched upward to claw at the ceiling.

Wait, RaLinWa motioned. *The Elders are here.*

They all stopped their frantic struggling. Down below, they saw a swarm of Elders thickly covering the floor of the chamber. In the center, a circle of Elders had surrounded the platform and they were furiously wrapping the Grand-Elders' shrouds in a sticky webbing.

Did you know they could do that? WaLiLa asked RaLinWa.

No, she motioned with a quick lift of her shoulders.

Dig, MalKai motioned again.

The Elders are going to figure it out, LorSenKiPe said. He motioned to a huddle of Elders near the entrance fluttering their limbs in rapid, panicked conversation.

They don't look like they have a plan, RaLinWa motioned in an uncharacteristic expression of dark doubt.

Then we follow MalKai's plan, WaLiLa motioned.

Their arms and legs were free, but their bodies were still trapped. They could not push themselves higher or drop down lower. So they all lifted two pairs of hands and worked to dig, but the surface of the ceiling was too smooth, as if bonded with some other substance. They banged their fists against the ceiling over and over until the surface shattered. They began to dig wildly, flinging chunks of dirt and petrified dew catcher root to the floor as they dug.

Where are we digging to? LorSenKiPe asked.

Dig, MalKai motioned again.

I don't think they are winning, RaLinWa motioned. They paused, looking down to see that the Grand-Elders' shrouds were starting to glow, making the Elders' webbing seem futile. The trainees returned to their work, digging more frantically. WaLiLa's hand touched something fleshy and her body jolted with hope.

WaLiLa wrapped both her feeling hands around the fleshy lump of dew catcher root.

Is it alive? MalKai asked.

WaLiLa tugged at it until the root pulsed, shifting from a pale whitish color to a deep purple.

Is that a dew catcher root? LorSenKiPe asked.

Yes. And we're going to take it out of here, RaLinWa motioned.

RaLinWa and MalKai began digging around the root, while WaLiLa kept a firm grasp on it.

When more of the root was cleared, WaLiLa jerked it free of the dirt and wrapped it around one of her wrists.

Hold tight, she motioned and lifted both her middle hands to grab a tighter hold. MalKai and RaLinWa quickly tapped their shoulders twice in prayer, then wrapped all six arms around WaLiLa making a round clump of their bodies.

Come on, Lor. Don't you want to escape? RaLinWa motioned when LorSenKiPe didn't join them.

LorSenKiPe circled his arms around them. He felt a pair of hands—he didn't know whose—reach out to grab him back.

Yank it, RaLinWa said.

WaLiLa surreptitiously reached out one of her lower hands and grabbed hold of one of the wings nearest her. Before anyone could protest, she heaved at the root with all her might. The root pulsed under her fingers, then retracted, hauling the four of them away from the Grand-Elders' chamber. They hurtled upward at an incredible speed, squeezing each other tight when they bumped into sharp rocks, crystals, and lumps of dead dew catcher root. No matter what they encountered—stinging worms, bulbous nests, chunks of ice—WaLiLa kept an unshakable grip on the root and the wing.

Breaking through the surface felt like one more fantastical twist in their mind-bending journey. They stood clustered together in the dew catcher's shadow and stared at each other in stunned stillness, waiting for the next disaster. But nothing around them warped or twisted, or melted into memory. It was day dark, they were standing at the edge of the fields, and they had escaped. WaLiLa let go of the root and they all watched it skitter across the dirt and whip against the stalk of the dew catcher it belonged to.

WaLiLa flicked her feeling hands from her waist to her chest. *We made it.*

They were so bruised and bloodied, they were barely recognizable. They examined each other's scratches and lumps and missing patches of skin. RaLinWa wiggled her fingers and rained them downward. *What is that?!?*

She pointed at WaLiLa and everyone turned to stare at the jagged scrap of wing in WaLiLa's hand.

You took a souvenir?!? LorSenKiPe motioned incredulously.

You... MalKai started an aggressive series of motions, but RaLinWa held her arms out, stopping all conversation. *It doesn't matter,* she motioned, her hands fluttering in discomfort. *We may never be safe again.*

* * *

There was a saying that everyone used in the fields. Any time disaster struck, some other pod stole your stash, your pod had a harder time collecting the day's nectar, you would lift one elbow vertically and fling it backward as if tossing it away. *The wing flings.*

WaLiLa had always taken the saying to mean that you can't control everything—some things are at the whims of the winds stirred up by the push and pull of wings. Now, in the aftermath of the Grand-Elders' invasion, she thought maybe *the wing flings* meant something else. As they stayed cocooned for two cycles, waiting for their bodies to heal, waiting for the Grand-Elders to reclaim them, waiting for the Elders to send for them, she thought maybe the wing flings meant that knowing the world—knowing the wing—would fling away everything you knew, fling you into a different you.

Their thirsts tampered and their fears raging, the four pod mates decided there was nothing to do but head back to the fields. They returned to the same tasks, but they were not the same workers. They wasted no energy bickering. WaLiLa could not even muster her long-standing animosity toward LorSenKiPe. Without friction or protest, they fell into a smooth cycle of rotating responsibilities, each of them taking turns to support the weight at the bottom and confront the stench at the top. Wings were out of the question, but perhaps they could secure leniency or escape a more severe punishment by collecting nectar with a new seriousness.

Once the work was done, they spent their free time sitting together in the fields, ripping off chunks of dew catcher stalk and tucking the stalk under their armpits, moving their arms lazily as they broke it down into a thick, drinkable liquid. There was nothing to be said that hadn't already been discussed during their healing. Now they spent their togetherness engulfed in the tense suspicion that their encounter with the Grand-Elders was not done.

The day the Grand-Elders came back for them was a day like any other. They were in the dew catcher fields, working without discussion or distraction. They reached the end of their row quickly and the tube—full of nectar—was a dark rusty orange.

Gathered around the collection tube, they worked together to drag it toward the nectar pool. As they neared the pool, its pulsing pushed at them like a gusty wind, vibrating not only their hearing membranes but their entire bodies. Tugging the collection tube forward, they tossed the opening of the collection tube into the pool. Once the tube connected with the pool, it yanked taut and gradually collapsed onto itself as the pool emptied it, leaving it soft and hollow. When the tube was completely limp, they scooped it up, hauled it back to the beginning of their row, and dropped it at the outer edge of the field.

We're done, RaLinWa motioned with a cascading clapping that traveled from the slap of her feeling hands against the palms of the middle hands down to her lower, and back up again. Her announcement was a mixture of relief and regret. The work, hard as it was, was the only thing—besides sleep—that could numb their worry.

A swirl of cold air surrounded them. They looked around frantically, their multi-lensed eyes searching the fields and each other's faces. Then the Grand-Elders' disembodied arms were there again, slowly taking shape in the work pod's minds. LorSenKiPe was tempted to hide in the burrow. RaLinWa was tempted to question them. MalKai was tempted to dig for another dew catcher root. And WaLiLa was tempted to run. But not one of them moved. Instead, they stood there shivering and cowering as their bodies were overtaken by a debilitating dread.

We have not traveled for so long, the Grand-Elders' arms motioned once they were completely formed. *We had hoped for more time to prepare you, but we underestimated the dedication of our offspring. They wish to protect you.*

After a few wingbeats of silence, everything inside the four pod members began to churn.

We will not harm you and we will bring you back home when we are done.

Great gusts of energy began to circulate through the four bodies at a ferocious pace. When they felt their bodies would burst, a tangle of purple threads erupted in each of their minds and they were engulfed in darkness.

In the darkness, they disassembled. Their bodies melted and they were horrified to feel themselves go liquid and disintegrate into shapeless blobs. There was a tiny pop, and each of them went hurtling—blind and numb—through the air. WaLiLa strained to see, but she had no eyes. She struggled to move, but she had no body. There was nothing but her consciousness and an insistent grinding sound following close behind her as she sped through an endless stretch of dark empty space. Incredulity, fear, and confusion suffocated her. She lost her grip on herself—unable to understand what was happening to her. In an intense implosion, she lost consciousness.

When she awoke, she was still an insignificant, deconstructed fleck of nothingness tumbling though the darkness. She lost consciousness over and over as the somersaulting through an endless, empty dark space continued—no rustling Grand-Elders, no whiplash of memory, and no hint of home. Then something changed. The air around her began to slowly thicken. She became aware of moisture plastering her skin. Before she even realized what she was doing, she began opening and closing her fingers. When she realized she had limbs again, she felt as if elation would split her in two. She kicked out, stretching and flexing her muscles, testing her range and strength.

In that clumsy experimental stretching, her arms bumped against her legs and torso. Terror washed over her when she discovered four of her arms were missing. Before she could give in to the agony of her loss, a loud pulsing exploded around her. The air around her—thickened to the point of liquidity—pressed inward, causing everything around her to tremble. She shot forward and the top of her head was shoved against a pliable surface. When the trembling passed, she was caught between relief and trepidation. She had a body! But the body was incomplete.

Suddenly the trembling resumed, shoving her harder, forcing her head into a flexible tunnel. The tunnel gripped her tightly, then rippled, pushing her body forward and guiding her head through a narrow opening. The motion stopped as suddenly as it began, and everything was new again. Where she had been tumbling through darkness, she now found herself surrounded by light. She was seized by another wave of trembling. Everything around her contracted and, in a rush of liquid, her body was thrust out of the tunnel and thrust into a world of thin, warm air.

At the outset, all she could see was her own tiny blood-splattered body. The body had strange, small hands and flat smooth skin. She was lifted into the air and distracted by a burst of pleasure as something wet rubbed against her body with a steady comforting rhythm. This was nothing like being yanked off the ground and being held—hovering in the air by the Grand-Elders. There was a softness to these movements as she was wrapped in something dry and cocoon-like before being placed in a pair of large moist arms.

A droplet of liquid splashed on WaLiLa's forehead. She was suddenly aware of a face hovering over her, dripping liquid from a large pair of eyes. The eyes—like her hands—were strange. She tried to lift her arms to her face to feel her own eyes, but found she had no control over her new limbs. They jerked up and down, twitching of their own volition.

She could do nothing but watch as more liquid collected in the large eyes overhead. She felt a conflicting sense of wonder as she worked to understand what was happening to her. She was aware too of a skittering panic that was erupting inside her, threatening her with suffocation. A distracting heat began to build inside the little body she was trapped in. An overwhelming urge began to tug at the body's mouth. The body's lips parted and, to WaLiLa's surprise, a piercing shriek came pouring out.

In that moment of confusion, the Grand-Elders' disembodied limbs broke into WaLiLa's brain again, reconstructing themselves in WaLiLa's mind.

You have arrived, the limbs motioned when they were complete. *Repeat after me.*

Severed from her body and with only a tenuous grip on her sanity, WaLiLa was too dumbfounded to comprehend the task. As the limbs motioned a jumble of words, WaLiLa watched in terror. When the arms stopped moving, WaLiLa remained still. An electrifying jolt of coldness shocked her.

REPEAT AFTER ME, the limbs demanded. The fear of returning to that dark dissolved state, prodded her to pretend— she pretended that she was intact, that she was calm enough to understand what the Grand-Elders wanted of her, that if she just obeyed, she would be safe. The limbs started to motion again and she wrestled herself into action. With an unwavering focus, she mimicked the shape of the disembodied arms with her own imagined limbs. She did not interpret; she did not decipher. She muted the churning of her mind and replicated until the disembodied arms were still.

When her mimicking was complete, the tangle of dark threads exploded within her again. They writhed around each other and wove themselves into thick ropes, snaking outward into the body that was sheltering her. WaLiLa watched as the threads sifted through the body's emotions and pinpointed a lump of sadness. She squirmed in horror as the threads wrapped the sadness in a cocoon of darkness and banked it inside her ephemeral form. When the threads withdrew, she was filled with a blindingly beautiful thrumming. Whatever form and consciousness was left of her dissolved into the intense pleasure of the vibrating emotion. The rustling of the Grand-Elders' breath rose around her, overlapping in a chorus of satisfied sighs.

In that instant—as she felt herself soaring—WaLiLa had a blast of clarity: Her life would never be useful to the Grand-Elders, not when they could use her body as a functional tool. She was both dew catcher and nectar collector, capturing emotion as if it were nectar and delivering it to the Grand-Elders for their consumption. Her pleasure was quickly extinguished. The wing flings, she thought—and fervently tried to cocoon herself against becoming completely destabilized. The dome, in all its drabness, seemed like a paradise compared to this captivity. She imagined the feathery softness of the wing in her hand. Though she knew it was useless, she worked to convince herself that if she tried hard enough, she could capture the pull of the wing and it would fling her back through the darkness that brought her to this terrifying limbo so that when she woke she would be safe and sound, a swarm of Elders passing overhead and nothing to look forward to but a million wingbeats of hard labor in the company of her work pod.

THE TAMING

Hunger throbbed between his eyes and echoed in his hollows. He was uneasy in his hide. Everything was emptiness and nothing changed. Sleep came in jagged spurts. When he woke, there was no leaping, no hunting, no wrestling. There were only the walls that he banged against until bruised.

The walls were wrong. He clawed them until they peeled, curling like a thin, shedding bark. But they were not made of bark, or stone, or water. They did not hold the bitter burn of urine, the musk of others, the stench of death. They were empty of scent and their fuzzy, moss-like surfaces carried the same dark hue as the rounded innards that spilled out of guts when he fed, when he fed.

When he tired, he rubbed against the walls, wearing away the fuzzy patterns in patches. He missed the trees. He missed the dirt, the sky, the river. Where had it all gone? Why was there no dirt to paw, no one to scent his scat, nowhere to run?

A whisper of feathers broke his world open again. He cocked his head. A blur of movement caused his fur to bristle. He crouched and lunged at the food, the flapping of wings. His jaws had closed around the feathered body before he knew what he was attacking.

A few seconds of familiarity: the dying prey screeching in his ears; the heat against his tongue; the hint of blood: food. Then everything flashed—dark, light, dark, then light again. Burning entered his paws and streaked through his legs. His body spasmed and he collapsed to the floor. He stretched toward the food, his tongue aching with want. He urged himself to scramble forward, but his muscles would not move. Blood seeped through feathers. The scent bloomed in his nostrils. He was flooded with agony. Then all was darkness.

Emptiness rippled through him. He shouldered the walls, but nothing changed. He was obsessive in his pacing, circling the space in a never-ending loop. Each time he crossed the place where the pain had felled him, a trace of odor wafted up from the floor. The scent of the wounded food plunged into him, inflaming his hunger again and again. He needed to feed.

The whisper of feathers again. He twisted into motion, his body a streak of speed. Before the room could flash—dark, light, dark, light—he lunged, severing the food's long neck. He was rewarded with thick wetness. Blood soaked his tongue. Then pain pulsed and snatched his body from his control. He whimpered and dropped to the floor, incapable of moving as the food staggered—headless and uneaten—across the space.

This time, when he heard the swish of feathers, he did not pounce. He squelched the instinct to spring toward the flapping, watching the food waddle around, his mouth drowning in saliva. He crept toward the food and nudged it with his snout. The warmth of its body soaked into the fur around his nose. He opened his jaws and hovered over the food, waiting. No pain. He closed his teeth gently on the food's body. Still the pain did not come.

He released the food and forced himself to the ground. He laid there, legs puddled around his empty belly, listening to his own sounds—the thumping of his heart, the gurgling of his stomach. He could not control the swelling of hunger in his chest. He could not stop the forward crawl, the sprawling in air. The room flashed dark, light, dark, light. But before the pain could level him, he fell on top of the food, blindly gouging and gnawing until his muscles seized and his body went slack.

A fleshy mound—pink and glistening—was there when he awoke. He crept toward the mound. It did not move. He nudged it with his nose. It shuddered, then was still. He licked it. Cold seeped into his tongue. His throat contracted with distaste. But hunger loomed. He opened his jaws and devoured.

The mound eaten, he stopped seeking. The air undulated around him in watery waves and he stumbled about, dulled and diminished. Each time the cold food appeared, he ate, then licked himself lazily, as everything sharp about him slouched into softness.

For a long stretch, there had been no cold food. He loped around, sniffing at corners and tripping over his paws until food—warm and flapping—fell from the ceiling. Odor invaded his nostrils. His mouth hurt with hunger. He remembered the warm blood against his tongue, the jerking of the prey against his jaws, but the instinct to attack was smothered by a throbbing in his joints. He skittered away from the warm food, pressing himself into a corner, to cower and rub his paws over his ears with each flutter.

Hunger roiled inside him. Sniffing at corners and walls led him nowhere. The wall made a loud scraping sound and started to separate. He hunched down and growled as the walls slid apart. He limped forward to investigate the new space and the scent of cold food exploded in his nostrils. He poked his head into the new space. He saw nothing—nothing new, nothing known.

The aroma of the food burrowed deeper into him and his hunger urged him onward. He bounded into the new space, sniffing at the floor. The cold food beckoned, but there were no other odors. He could not scent trees, soil, or water. He sniffed at the walls, but nothing known was there—just more mossy patterns in its wrong color. He ran, feeling the impact of his paws against the floor vibrate through his limbs. Running triggered kinetic memories: the thrill of the hunt, the ecstasy of the pounce, the satisfaction of the capture. His mouth grew wet. He gnashed his teeth, frantic to feel the rip of flesh, crunch of fang against bone.

There was no prey, but there was a mound of cold food. He leapt at it and gobbled until his tongue went numb.

The space for running seemed endless. He ran just to feel the push and pull of his muscles. He ran through the tenderness he felt in his paws. He ran through the creaking and popping of his joints. In the running, he felt a whisper of the feral freedom he had lost.

In the running, he scented something new in the air, something known. He threw his head back, and howled. A howl came echoing back. He shot forward, hurling himself toward the sound. A silhouette in the narrow space ahead. Another of him standing steady and calm. He slowed to a trot up and sidled close. She licked his face and pranced as he sniffed at her neck, down her back. When he had the scent of her, she yipped and took off running. He sprinted behind her, then matched her stride. Bodies stretching and gliding together, keeping pace at another's hip—this was known.

He smelled the rank odor before she changed course. She veered away from the long open space and he careened to a stop. He could hear her yipping, calling him to her, but he could not see her. He leapt forward toward her sounds, and immediately scrambled back when he smelled that odor—rank and redolent. She yipped again and he hunkered down, crawling toward her, into a different space, teeth bared, ears flattened, shoulders hunched, growling at the bad scent, a spear of warning hanging in air.

The other of him charged at him, nipping him on the shoulder. Shoving him toward a mound of cold food. He turned away, sniffing at the floor in search of that smell, the source of that odor that alerted him to danger. She butted him in his side, pushing his snout toward the cold food. His mouth moistened. Even though his gut did not urge, it had become known. He consumed it all, cold bite by cold bite.

Sprawled, slack-limbed and dulled, he scented a new odor: sweet, sharp, not known. As he lay there, dazed and urgeless, a new thing toddled around him on shaky legs. It was fur-less and paw-less. It had a little glistening mouth that made gurgling sounds. He raised his head to sniff at the little wrong paws. A growl rumbled from behind him. He looked over to see the other of him baring her teeth at him. She strained toward him, but she could not pounce. She was held back by two living things. They towered over her like small trees and barked at each other with choppy, indecipherable sounds. The desire to flip over and crouch low at the ready rolled through him. He started a snarl, but the sound died out before it could gather any strength. The new thing wandered away, trailing a string of tiny noises, and he was powerless to do anything but lay there, twitching with alarm, as darkness came to claim him again.

When he woke, one of the tall ones was touching him with its wrongness. Like the toddling new thing, the tall one had no fur and no claws. He was too weak to even snap at the tall one when it pushed him to the floor, stretched out his tail, prodded his legs, pushed against his belly, pressed its odd head against his chest. He shook himself as hard as he could, but his limbs only shivered. He felt his back leg lift. There was pressure on his soft parts. Another tall one lifted his head and cradled his jaw, wrapped its clawless paws around his maw and forced his mouth open. When it put its wrong paw against his tongue and touched his teeth, he gagged on that terrible scent. His stomach clenched and a hoarse hacking broke out in his throat. The two tall ones barked at each other then released him.

The other of him was loud. Her yipping echoed in his ears. She circled the tall ones, nipping at their feet, prodding them toward the wall. At the wall, she pushed her head against a dark spot, then turned back to the tall ones. She nudged their clawless paws, until they leaned against the wall. She trotted back and forth between the tall ones as they pushed and pushed. When the wall split under their pushing, she ran over to him and bit his side. Then she ran back to the tall ones. Bright light flowed from the split in the wall. She yelped, ran into the light, and disappeared. He climbed to his feet and loped toward the tall ones. They didn't move. He ducked his head, skittered past them, leaving behind their putrid odor and the wrongness of no escape.

Warmth. He inhaled. A crispness seared his lungs. He craned his head back and scented odors around him: earth, leaf, tree, food—warm food. A cacophony of images flashed through his mind: branches stirring in the wind, the undulation of a river flowing quietly, a flock of feathered food cutting a shadow across the sky. He lowered his head and sniffed at the dirt. He scented urine, insects, feces. It was all known. He looked back at the bad place where he had been trapped. The other of him leapt at him. She hooked her paws around his neck and they tumbled over. Then she was up, nipping at his hide before scampering away.

He watched the flash of her haunches as she leapt into a cluster of bushes. He plunged in after her watching as she buried her face in the bush, gnashing berries between her teeth. Snatched a bundle of berries from its branches. Dropped them at his feet. Berries were not known as food. She nosed the berries toward him. Hunger pressed at his ribs. He scooped up the berries. Fangs pierced skin. Plant juices seeped into his mouth and swelled on his tongue. He swallowed. A loud howl tore loose from his throat without him commanding it to.

The other of him bit his shoulder and ran off. He licked his chops and followed. He ran beneath leafy overhangs and jumped over fallen trees. Foliage brushed his sides. His fur tingled. He lost himself in the flash of color around him. Then a yelp. A screech. He slowed. She tumbled to the ground, a small struggling body clamped in her jaws. She dropped it in the dirt. He backed away. She clamped a warm limb in her mouth. Severed it from the body. The scent filled his nostrils. She dropped the limb before him, then sat licking her paws. He paced back and forth, looking at the fresh kill splayed in the dirt. When he did not feed, she dragged the carcass to him and stood over it, urging him to eat. Scent exploded in his skull. He hungered. He dipped his head down and bit into its side. The hide resisted, then released. Blood swelled in his mouth. Everything became a blur as the gorging engulfed all his senses. When the food was nothing more than head and paws, hide and bones, they lay in the dirt, heads lolling, drifting slowly into sleep's embrace.

She left a trail of scent for him to follow. It led him to downward sloping land that was soft and moist underfoot. He spied her head and shoulders cutting across a wide rippling river. He dove in after. Water soaked his fur, washed away the remains of cold-food haze. The other of him emerged, dripping, on the other side. She climbed onto the rocky bank and disappeared behind a great stream of water. He paddled harder, fighting the churning of the water to scramble up the rocks.

He scented her in a small dry space behind the falling water. Inside, the light was soft, dappled by the falling water. Inside, the slamming of the water echoed against the walls. Loping toward her, he remembered other walls, mossy walls that triggered endless circling with no escape. The ghost of pain daggered around inside him. He turned away, scrambling toward light. She tackled him before he could exit. Nuzzled his cheeks. Licked across his forehead, behind his ears. The pull of her tongue soothed him. The soft parts of him shifted. He yipped softly and fell into a heap at her feet.

When he returned the licking, moisture collected on his tongue. He continued, nipping across her shoulders, grooming her down her back. At her tail, her scent blossomed. The sounds around him amplified—his ears were filled with her panting, the pounding of water, the rustling of his own breath. He circled her, stopping at her haunches. A flicker of memory tugged at him: his pack lying about; the leader of his pack thrusting behind another. His soft parts grew heavy and hard.

He entered her, the water rumbling in his ears. Heat, rose from her body. Heat, rose within him. His thrusting becoming a thundering. The movement of muscle shook loose all forgetting. He knew then that he was lone. Splintered from his pack. He had no one to kill with, no one to run with, no one to punish his errors. He was alone with the furious water; alone with the other of him; alone, knowing that he had become unknown to himself.

The coupling done, they lapped sweat from each other's fur until they could separate. The scent was faint, but he could smell it from beyond the water—one of their own. She streaked past him, barking and bounding back and forth on the rocks at the edge of the water. Across the water, a tall one was pacing. It held the wrong scent, it held their scent. He growled. Nudged her toward the dry space, toward safety, but she did not heed him. She dove off the rocks and plunged into the water. He jumped in after, racing toward the moist earth on the other side.

They climbed out of the water, but the tall one had gone, trailing layers of odor, both its own putrid scent and their familiar one. She ran along the scent, leaping over logs and rocks. He ran at her hip, skirting trees, dodging bushes and branches. He halted when the bad place was in sight, his chest grew tight. That rank odor rolled toward him. She bounded right up to the bad place, racing back and forth, barking at its closed walls.

When the bad place opened, he turned tail, ducking into

the greenery. He watched a tall one appear in the opening. A low growl vibrated in his throat. The tall one held one of their own—small, not fully grown—captured in its arms. The captured one whined, stretching toward the other of him, pushing against the tall one with long, gangly legs. The other of him pawed the dirt, keening in uneven guttural tones. She crept close. He growled and shot out of the bushes. Darted forward and pushed her away. The tall one dropped a mound of cold food on the ground, then disappeared into the bad place, carrying the captured one into the darkness. Its high-pitched yipping echoed from the bad place. She bared her fangs at him, then crouched over the cold food and ate. He licked her face, watching the dullness climb into her eyes.

She crawled toward the bad place and lay in front of the opening. She tucked her tail between her legs, buried her head in her paws. A clawless paw emerged and grabbed the back of her neck. The tall ones leaned over her, throwing their shadows across her fur. Her tail, lifted; her soft parts, examined; her belly prodded, then the tall ones moved away.

When he saw the clawless paws again, they were freeing two, three, five captured ones to scamper around the other of him. They tumbled over her, nipping at each other's fur, jumping over each other's limbs, pawing at each other's bodies. He crept closer to watch them—the beginnings of a pack—surround her. The walls of the bad place began to close. He scrambled backward, then darted forward when she ran into the opening. They licked each other restlessly. He inhaled her scent. A clawless paw yanked her backward. He howled. Then he ran.

HEMMIE'S CALENTURE

Barataria, Louisiana, 1814

A Surprise Salvation

Hemmie's skin was feverish and slick with sweat. Everything seemed to bend and stretch and warp around her. Breathing had never felt like this, like it was taking every ounce of her strength to keep air in her lungs, to keep her alive. It was as if the wet thickness of the swamp was suffocating her. Not just the air, everything—the whispering of vines, the rustling of frogs, the writhing of snakes— was pulsing and squeezing tighter and tighter around her.

She had forgotten where she was running to—each new dark thicket of trees looked like the last. She stumbled forward, slowly becoming aware that she was no longer running, she was hobbling along, pushing herself onward and away with the sounds of the swamp ringing in her ears.

Suddenly it seemed as if the earth tilted. She grabbed at the air then somehow found her footing. She urged herself on, haunted by the dogs, their barking, the flash of their teeth as they panted hot on her heels.

Won't be long now, she thought, certain that with every ragged excruciating inhale, she was welcoming death.

In quick flashes she saw everything that had not gone according to plan: the dog's jaws clamped onto her leg; Nenah's arms trembling as she raised the tree branch to bludgeon the dog again and again; her mangled leg, an embarrassment of exposed flesh and gutted muscle after Nenah had had pried the dog's jaws open to free her.

Won't be long now. It wouldn't be long now before Nenah was caught. Before the dogs led the bounty men to her. *To my dead body*, she corrected herself. Her body was afire with contradictory sensations—total numbness, yet every limb was tingling with excruciating ache and exhaustion. She stopped at a small crooked creek and tottered at the water's edge. On the other side, a riotous thicket of sweetflag beckoned.

With nothing but rest on her mind, she plunged into the creek, pain spiking as she splashed through the weak current. She climbed up the opposite bank and nested down in the tall craggy grass. Death had not done its duty. At home, death was a sudden force, swooping into villages unannounced, feeding without reason, and barreling away before anyone could call its name. Here—in this bitter land—death fed slowly, snacking on your spirit, fiddling with your sanity, sipping from your soul. It became a worm in the flesh, burrowing in deeply to delight in your destruction, in the maiming of neighbors, the burying of children, the disfiguring of your own worthless flesh.

"How much longer?" she pleaded aloud, knowing that death would not answer. Ever since she had been yanked from her life, death had gone mute. It did not heed her during her neverending walk to the coast. It laughed at her prayers when she was chained in the bowels of the great ship. It took others during the branding of flesh, the shaming of souls, the flogging of skin, the humiliation of rape, but no matter how many horrors of captivity she suffered, death refused her.

A flash of light exploded over her head and she was filled with a rush of relief. *It won't be long now.* But her vision did not go black. Nor did the light extinguish her breath. Instead, it rained down in a spray of sparks. Hemmie stared upward, eyes widening as the sparks joined to form a long streak that cut through the air and split itself in two. The light streaked through the muggy night air, snaking around in spirals, slowly shaping itself into the outline of a figure.

Fear took Hemmie into its mouth and she shrank away as the figure reached outward as if to embrace the night. Tiny winged things—gnats, midges, and mosquitoes—clogged the air, colliding with the light. Upon contact, they burst into spark, transforming the air above Hemmie's head into a shower of twinkling lights. When Hemmie dared to look, she saw that the light had formed into a masked woman wearing a beaded dress that emitted a soft glow.

"Close your eyes," the woman said. Her words did not touch the air, instead they rustled through Hemmie's mind.

Hemmie stared up at her, frozen in incomprehension and disbelief. The woman's hair was covered with a wooden antelope crown; a curtain of beads hid her face. She leaned forward and touched the top of Hemmie's head. A soft tingling spread from her scalp to the rest of her body, soaking into Hemmie's skin and claiming her fever. The pain that had been shooting through her body dissolved.

"Close your eyes," the woman said again, the rustling of her voice louder and more forceful.

Hemmie obeyed, but the moment her eyelids met, she swooned as if the muddy earth beneath her was shifting. She flicked her eyes open, but nothing had changed. She was still sheltered in sweetflag with a glimmering apparition menacing her overhead. Hemmie stared up at her helplessly.

"Do as I say," the woman rustled loudly.

Hemmie squeezed her eyes shut.

"Find a safe place. See it in your mind."

Hemmie fought to comply, but the daily brutality had done its work. The word 'safety'—like 'home'—had been buried deep. What flickered to mind easily was the opposite of safety—rows of battered heads rotting on poles, severed fingers discarded among tree roots, raw gashes where tongues and ears should have been, ropy scars that transformed skin into bumpy expanses of rigid, shiny knots. Suddenly the gruesome memories collapsed and withered. In an instant, she was thrown back into her seven-year-old body. Terrified but determined, she was climbing into an armoire armed with the childish certainty that she could call death.

The darkness soothed her as she snuggled into the clean clothes she had just stacked neatly at the bottom of the armoire. Clutched to her chest, she held a pilfered chunk of warm bread and a rum bottle full of an ominous dark liquid studded with herbs. She could feel the glassy kiss of the bottle as she guzzled its contents, gobbled the bread, and lay there, motionless, waiting for death to help her escape. It was sleep—not death—that came for her tiny body. Even as a child, death did not heed her. She slept off the poison in the nest of clothes, blissfully dreaming of rolling green hills, fruit trees, and her parents' arms. It was that fleeting moment of safety—the only one she could recall—that she was clinging to when her damaged body was lifted into air, pulled up from the swamp as if a rope was tied to her chest, and hurled into weightless nothingness.

Solitude, Ruined

Hemmie's eyelids fluttered. She felt herself go slick as Nenah's hand gripped her thigh. She hooked her hands over Nenah's shoulders and pulled her closer. Hemmie lost her footing and they tumbled to the ground, Nenah's blue-black lips pressed against Hemmie's neck.

"Come here."

Those two words reverberated through Hemmie's dream, halting the cane leaves whipping in the wind over her and Nenah's heads. She opened her eyes, shot up to sitting, and looked around. Her bedroom was dark and empty. She fell back onto the mattress, threw a pillow over her face, and closed her eyes again. Nenah was there, her dress sticky with sweat and her hand outstretched. Hemmie willed herself to feel Nenah's touch again, but she could not reinsert herself into the tangle of Nenah's arms.

Hemmie kicked at the twisted bed sheets, then went stiff as a cramp seized her calf. She gritted her teeth and pounded her leg with her fists. Where it should have been deformed and tattered, the skin was magically smooth. She did not deny the miracle, but this flesh was not her flesh. What had been gnawed into uselessness by the dogs should not have been able to be replaced by a fully functioning limb. It was attached to her body, but Hemmie did not trust it. She resented its presence, and hated the way it was almost always screeching with pain.

Hemmie scrambled to the edge of her bed, parted the mosquito netting, and reached for the glass carafe on her nightstand. The rustling of the two words—"Come here"—echoed in her mind again. She threw her head back and pressed the carafe to her lips, guzzling until her chest was warm and she could cram no more liquid down her throat.

Slowly, she pulled her bonnet off her head and her hands fell heavy into her lap. She did not need light to know that every branch of every tree in the fruit grove outside her bedroom window was empty. She could mark the passage of time by the amount of misbeliefs and cumquats left on the tress. Now the trees were barren. Her stomach growled, gurgling for something fresh. Sitting in the darkness, wracked with hunger, she was taken, whip-fast, back to the bowels of the ship. The all-consuming need to feed was but one of the terrors she had survived on the journey far from home. There were the sores where the shackles had bit into her wrists and ankles, leaving behind a ghostly scarring. The incessant itch of being always moist with feces and urine. The caking of blood and vomit. The nearness of death. The howling of those losing their sanity, their holiness, their breath.

Hemmie leaned over the bed and shoved her hand beneath the mattress. She clutched the hilt of the knife she slept on every night and withdrew it. Its weight was satisfying and solid in her palm. She laid the blade flat against her chest.

"I am coming to you," she whispered to her parents in her mother tongue.

Lightning-quick, she flipped the hilt outward, pointing the blade at her belly. She tightened her grip and thrust the knife inward, but her arms seized. The hilt burned her fingers as if aflame. She dropped the knife and those two words rustled in her mind again.

"Come here."

Hemmie clapped her hands over her ears and swung her legs out of bed. Her knife tumbled to the floor. A yell of rage on her lips, she rushed out of her bedroom, down the hall, through the kitchen, and into the living room, but there was nowhere she could go to escape. Everything around her was due to the glimmering woman who had snatched her away from the promise of death. The rising of the sun each time her body crossed into the foyer. The house itself, that began shifting its wooden planks the moment she crossed the threshold to step out of the front door and stand in the perpetually dawning light. Hemmie stepped onto the dirt clearing outside her front door, listening to the explosion of loud clacking as the back of the house collapsed, the walls and floorboards separating from their joints and stacking themselves in a neat pile like a folded fan. She could not avoid thinking of the woman made of light every time her rooms and hallways ceded their structure, creaking loudly as they deconstructed from a dwelling into an unassuming armoire.

This place was made of that woman's magic. Her little patch of paradise—which centered around a haphazard jumble of chiffarobes, dressers, vanities, and etargés—was yanked straight from her childhood memory and imbued with powers she had never imagined. But rather than celebrate her good fortune, Hemmie tried to shove it away. She started her mornings standing in front of a pale yellow cupboard studded with little glass knobs. Whenever its speckled paint stayed put rather than swam before her eyes, she would tug the cupboard open and grab a bottle at random from the collection of alcohol stashed within. This morning, her ritual was ruined by those two words that would not quit their rustling in her mind. She drank, squinting at the sun while the burn of alcohol spread from her throat to her chest. A bottle could start to deaden the memories that plagued her, but it did nothing to quell the woman's rustling.

"Come here."

This time the words were accompanied by an insistent force tugging at her navel. She tried to return the bottle to the cupboard, but the tugging jerked her backward and the bottle slipped from her hand, shattering in the dirt. The tugging dragged her away from the jumble of furniture, across an open field, and into her barren fruit grove. The grassy earth beneath her feet, rose and fell gently, rolling with each footfall. She stopped struggling and followed the tugging. She ducked beneath the branches of trees stripped of fruit and hopped over a clean stream empty of fish. It had been thrilling to discover that nothing in her lush domain would rot or die, and just as crushing to learn that nothing could blossom or grow here either. Even so neutered, she had determined she would sooner deal with gnawing hunger than re-enter the world that had chewed her to bits. She would stay hidden there, and lick her wounds in blessed isolation until death finally came for her.

"Stop," the voice rustled.

Hemmie halted under the boughs of a broad oak tree. She pressed her ear against the tree's gnarled bark as if it had secrets to share, but the tree was silent.

"Dig," the voice rustled, and she felt herself dragged down to her knees. The roughness of the dirt pressed against her palms, she tried to force herself back up to standing, but her body would not cooperate. Even her bones seemed to be straining toward the dirt. She relented and laid flat on her belly.

"Dig," the voice rustled again.

Hemmie watched helplessly as her plump, dark fingers

plunged into the dirt. Once in the dirt, her hand was still, as if whatever force had been controlling her had run out of power. She took up the task, plunging her fist downward, pushing deeper and deeper into the earth. Suddenly, her fingers touched air. She yanked her hand back in surprise and squinted through the hole. Before she could see anything, the tugging sensation returned. Wrapping around both wrists, it guided her hands into the hole she had dug. When both hands were shoved into the opening, she could feel her forearms pushing against the dirt, spreading the hole into a yawning gap. There was a tiny pop, then a stream of mosquitos flew upward from the hole and swarmed her face. She swiped at her face with her shoulder and instantly recoiled.

When a briny blast of swamp air smacked against her skin, she leaned into the hole and was shocked to discover that her undulating patch of land was hovering in air, floating above the very same spread of swamp where the glimmering woman had found her. From over twelve feet above, she could hear owls ruffling their feathers in preparation for night hunting and the whisper of Spanish moss as the wind whipped through the treetops. The croaking of the frogs, the swelling of birdcalls, it all swirled upward, reaching toward Hemmie in a cacophony of sound.

She exhaled and laid her head on her forearms. The movement of the swamp below was soothing. The lazy drift of a water moccasin displacing floating duckweed in a murky river lulled her into relaxation. Just beyond the stretch of swamp she could comfortably see, a burst of light exploded. She leaned further into the opening and strained to look down. When the burst of light became a tiny whirling tornado, Hemmie was slow to react. In a flash, the light took to the sky. It flew straight up at Hemmie, shooting through the hole to slam into her forehead. She scrambled backward, the woman's rustling cackling in her ears.

"No more hiding for you," the woman rustled in Hemmie's mind.

Hemmie leaned back onto her elbows, eyes darting around as she waited for whatever terrors the whirling light had in store for her.

"Do you feel that?" the woman rustled.

At first, Hemmie felt nothing. Then she was blinded by an intense headache that erupted in the middle of her head and sent a searing pain straight down her spine.

"This pain is yours," the woman rustled, "I'll release you from it when you bring yourself to me."

Hemmie flipped over and piled the dirt back into the hole. The woman's warning whispering in her ears, Hemmie climbed to her feet and rushed back to her menagerie of furniture. She returned to the pale yellow cupboard and guzzled more alcohol, pausing to see if the pain would fade. Her vision went blurry with the drink, but the pain carried on unabated. She pressed her palms against her scalp as the pain flitted from her forehead down into her sinuses and outward toward her ears.

For a few seconds, the pain was blinding and all she could do was grip the cupboard as it pounded mercilessly through her skull. When the intensity subsided, she stumbled over to a squat white vanity with curved legs. The top drawer, when slide open, revealed a collection of shriveled animal parts in small glass jars. These objects—opossum tail, shrew fur, and other animal remains—had been her only medicine since she was marooned on her island of green. For the headache, she selected three jars holding large hard-shelled beetles, hoping their bitterness would counter the pain.

Head still throbbing, she dumped the insects into a small pouch and pummeled it with her fat fingers. The pouch tucked in her fist, she pointed her index finger at the sky and started to bark loudly. After four barks, water began to flow from her fist. Once it was soaking wet, she lowered her arms and massaged the pouch until the pulverized bugs were transforming into a moist, pliable mush.

"Leave me alone," she yelled, rolling the mush into a ball and shoving it between her teeth and cheek. The mush dissolved in her mouth and her whole body went limp as the pain fled her body. The moment the pain disappeared, so did the inebriation. Suddenly she could feel the roar of her hunger, shaking her body with its rumbling. She frowned. With the fruit and fish disappeared, her hunger was nothing more than an annoyance. Leaving the white vanity behind, she trudged over to a tall, mahogany chifferobe. She placed one hand flat against its side and willed the wood to heat under her touch. After a few minutes, the scent of freshly baked bread wafted from the chifferobe.

Hemmie grabbed a length of linen from the neighboring cupboard and plucked a perfect loaf from the top shelf. She leaned on the chifferobe and fed herself small, pleasureless chunks of bread. As soon as the bread was done, the pain rebounded, pulsing at the base of her neck and scaling her scalp in an unstoppable expansion across her hairline, before diving deep into her skull. She let out a yell.

"Come here!" The rustling of the woman's voice was firm.

Hemmie banged her fist against the chifferobe. Her hand itched for the knife that she had been unable to use.

"There is no such thing as salvation," she thought bitterly. She looked around at the land that had—for brief flashes of time—gifted her with a sensation she imagined must be akin to freedom. She reached her hand out toward the fruit grove without knowing what she was reaching for. She let her hand drop and slap, limp, against her thigh. None of this had ever really been hers, and now she could not even pretend this was her home.

The Journey Below

Hemmie looked down at her nightgown. Across the chest and down her thighs, the fabric was soiled with grass stains and dirt. She couldn't imagine how she could obey—would she shove herself through the hole and plummet through the air, her soiled nightgown flapping around her? She returned to her doorstep. Whatever she was going to face, she would need reinforcements. Her hand made contact with the armoire and the house hurriedly clacked itself into place, firming up its structure as she stepped into the parlor. She tried to outpace her dread, marching to her bedroom with a haste intended to leave all thought behind. Her fingers shook as she pulled off the nightgown and tugged on a pair of wool stockings. She paused to grab a leather sheath from the nightstand drawer. She worked hard to steady her hands as she recovered the knife from the floor, lashed the sheath to her lower leg, and slipped the knife into the holster.

So armed, she stretched a thin shift over her fleshy body and tied two petticoats on top. A pair of heavy boots went on her feet and a dark traveling dress covered her body. She tossed a white capelet over her shoulders and slapped a day cap over her hair. She bristled at the burden of the clothes but the pounding of her headache pushed her to press on. Muttering assurances to herself, she tied the straps of her cap tightly under her chin and stomped back down the hall.

When she stepped out of the house, it was with the somber air of a woman headed to the stockades. Back at the pale yellow cupboard, she grabbed a flask from the top shelf and filled it with liquor from one of the many bottles in her stash. The flask, she tucked in her pocket, then returned to the mahogany chifferobe, willing it to bake three perfect loaves of bread. The bread, she stuffed in a pouch that she strapped to her waist. In a dark cherry etargé, she located a rifle, holster, and ammunition. The rifle, she slipped into its holster, which she strapped to her back.

After bundling the ammunition into a pack she tied to her hip, she felt that tugging sensation claim her hands again. She tried to close the etargé, but her hands thrust themselves forward, grasping at air.

"Grab the rope, my pet," the woman rustled in her mind.

Hemmie clenched her fists and fought to hold her hands still. Was this to be her future? The moment her mind wandered, her hands flew forward and picked up a long length of rope. She watched helplessly as her hands wrapped the rope around her waist, knotting it tight before winding its length around and around until the rope was snug against her waist. After her fingers had tucked in the loose ends of the rope, the tugging disappeared. She stood in front of the ramshackle jumble of furniture and trembled. Her body was heavy with provisions—the full flask, the pouch bulging with bread, the weaponry strapped to her body, but she did not feel fortified. She felt as raw and indentured as she had before she escaped. The tugging sparked up again and she let loose a howl, then rushed to the oak tree hoping her compliance would erase the need for the woman to steal away her self-control.

At the oak tree, she fell to her knees with no hesitation and made quick work of digging the dirt out of the hole again. The swamp below was as it had been, muggy and swelling with sound.

"Here," the woman rustled and Hemmie felt a tingling in her

ankles. Working to avoid becoming the woman's living puppet, Hemmie shifted her body around and shoved her tingling ankles into the hole. She seized up, waiting for the fall, but nothing came. Looking down, she saw that she was stuck at the knees. She kicked at the earth, softening the dirt with the prodding of her calves and shins. Slowly, the hole widened. She pitched downward, jerking to a stop as the dirt pressed against her hips. A few more kicks and gravity grabbed hold of her, yanking her through the hole. She plummeted, her skirts ballooning to slow her fall. When her body began to list back and forth like a leaf, she exhaled. Then her hands, returned to the woman's command. With no permission from Hemmie, her hands freed the loose ends of the rope.

"Up," the woman rustled and Hemmie's hands shot overhead, the ends of the rope firmly in her grasp. A fierce wind surged around her, throwing her into a dizzying spin. The rope undulated around her like tentacles, unfurling as she spun.

"Now," the woman rustled the moment Hemmie's body reached the treetops. Her hands flung outward, throwing the ends of the rope away from her body. The rope split the air, whistling as it streaked through foliage and wrapped around thick tree branches. As a reflex, Hemmie grabbed two fistfuls of rope and shrieked as the ropes pulled taut, skinning her palms. Once the plummeting halted, Hemmie's body jerked to an abrupt stop and the woman's tingling abandoned her.

She hung in air, suspended between her island of green overhead and the swamp below. Directly below her was a large, spiky fern and a few patches of cotton grass. She began to gasp for air as the pressure of the rope tugging at her waist became more and more intense. She let go of the rope, loosened the knot, and scrunched into a ball. She was overtaken by panic in her tumble to the ground.

The Passion Flowers and the Bear

Hemmie was examining the ripped skin on her palms when a sweet heady scent exploded in her nostrils. With each inhale, she was filled with a soft, soaring euphoria. She patted the food sack at her waist, jostled the flask in her pocket, and checked the holsters at her back and calf. Satisfied that everything was secured, she sniffed the air, following the intoxicating scent right into a patch of dense foliage. She thought of nothing but the potent smell as she pushed past all manner of branch, leaf, and bush. The scent seemed to double at a cypress tree where Hemmie noticed clusters of passionflower winding around the tree's trunk.

The tall green stamen at the flower's center captivated Hemmie. Something about the contrast of its unadorned erectness as it protruded high above a full skirt of long lavender petals made Hemmie smile. The flower's colorful contradictions—a powdery blast of red exploded above each petal—seemed to insist that that which had been destroyed could emerge into fullness again.

Hemmie had the wild thought that these flowers, with their ridiculous riot of color, could heal her. She snuck a glance over her shoulder and flipped open the flaps of her capelet. Unbuttoning the top three buttons of her bodice, she bared her chest. The flowers—plucked from the vine and tucked against her chest—bathed her in coolness before sending a soporific buzz through her muscles to slowly seep into her cells. Her limbs loosened and she felt the nagging dissatisfaction that dragged her down daily wash away.

She was reclasping her dress when a rank scent engulfed her. Trembling with alarm, Hemmie turned and saw a large dark blur crashing through the foliage. She darted around the cypress tree and sprang into a sprint, quickly considering the scalability of each plant she raced past. None of them—not the cottonwood, magnolia tree, or dewberry bush—would bear her weight. She stopped short at a black gum tree and launched herself at its trunk. The lightheadedness of the passionflowers still whipping through her, she shimmied upward, grabbing onto branches and struggling to drag her heft up the trunk and onto the tree's higher branches.

When she could climb no higher, she settled herself into a deep crook between the trunk and a thick branch. Gasping for breath, she looked down to see a black bear standing on its hind legs, gouging at the tree bark below. Hemmie leaned her head back against the tree trunk and closed her eyes. Tightening her jaw, she worked to draw storm clouds toward her.

"You can't control the weather down here, my pet."

Hemmie opened her eyes. She was alone and the sky overhead was clear with not a cloud in sight.

"What do you want?" Hemmie asked aloud.

"I want," the woman rustled, "to see what you can do."

Hemmie looked down. The bear was still there, clawing at the base of the tree. She felt the rifle pushing against her spine, but she did not reach for it—she would not have an innocent animal's death on her hands. She considered diving forward and tumbling to the ground, but even with her history she could not convince herself that death by mauling was a wise solution to her misery. She tightened her grip on the tree and launched down a forgetting spell. She had invented it during her long days of solitude, intending to erase her past, but any memories she succeeded in disappearing always returned the next morning with an inexhaustible malice and vigor. The forgetting spell was not a permanent solution to the bear either. When the spell hit, the bear fell backward, looked around as if confused, then shook its head vigorously and resumed its attack.

"We have so much work to do," the woman rustled.

Suddenly Hemmie's throat was gripped by an ululation. Along with the vibrating sound, a swelling thickened in her throat until she felt she would suffocate.

"Relax," the woman rustled as Hemmie sputtered, coughing and frantically gasping for breath. Eruptions of red mist shot from her mouth with each cough. The mist went rolling down the tree trunk to drape over the bear's head. The bear snuffled and backed away, flattening a young cherry laurel in its retreat. The mist collected into a huge clump, expanding into a big, bulky shape twice the bear's size. The bear crouched and bellowed, an explosion of deep, throaty sound that shook Hemmie to her core, then it turned and lumbered away. Hemmie gripped the tree, watching the bear's head rising and falling with each of its long, loping strides. In the animal's absence, the mist dispersed, thinning until it vanished in air.

A Debt to Be Repaid

By the time the fountain of sparks burst through the air, announcing the woman's return, Hemmie was depleted of resistance. She shut her eyes. She did not want to see the sizzling lines of light curving under, over, and around each other to form the shape of her tormentor.

"You are a selfish one, aren't you?" the woman rustled after her body had fully formed.

Hemmie slowly opened her eyes. The woman was hovering just

out of reach, her body gleaming and her face hidden behind the fringe of beads.

"You have enjoyed all the blessings I have bestowed upon you, yet you refuse to come when I call. It is time for you to pay your debt."

Hemmie winced. She hadn't asked the woman to save her. To have to pay her back for a favor she didn't want made her situation feel worse.

"I have need of an army," the woman rustled. "You must raise a battalion a few hundred strong."

Every part of Hemmie clenched. She would sooner cut off her own hands than surround herself with people. She did not want to know ten people, let alone hundreds. People were nothing but poison and a burden; she had no use for them.

"Are you asleep?" the woman rustled when Hemmie did not answer.

Hemmie gripped the tree so hard, she felt her fingers would go numb.

"I..." she said and fell silent. The whole thing was ridiculous. She was no commander, she was nothing but a runaway.

"While you are hiding from me, do you know what's happening? The British are circling in their ships. They've burned this nation's capital and they're moving south towards you right now."

"The British?" Hemmie said. She stared at the woman. There had been bitter arguments in the months before Hemmie and Nenah escaped about what it meant that the British were attacking. News had spread of skirmishes with Canadian armies in the north and with the natives of this land in the west, so many armies eager to beat back the Americans with the support of the British. Some of the enslaved wanted to join the British too, ready to do anything that would make them free.

"The plantations along the river are filled with able-bodied men. Go there and find my army."

At the word plantation, Hemmie went stiff.

"I'll never go back there," she whispered.

"You have me now," the woman rustled, the long fringe of her beaded skirt clattering loudly.

Hemmie could feel the panic gnawing at her.

"Can't you just make an army?" she asked.

"Out of thin air?" the rustling deepened into a sound Hemmie realized must have been laughter. "No, I need something to work with."

Hemmie frowned. She hadn't escaped captivity for this. She and Nenah were supposed to be together in the swamp—or die trying. Instead, death had eluded her again.

"Do not despair. This is a battle you will want to win," the woman rustled. She waved her hand in the air and left behind a streak of sparks. The sparks coalesced into a map that Hemmie did not even recognize as land.

"This is where we are," the woman rustled, pointing to a spot on the map. "And this," she said pointing to a large dark splotch that pulsed west of the swamp, "is our enemy."

'*Our* enemy?' Hemmie wanted to snap, but the dark spot was menacing, filling her with a cold terror.

"What is that?" she asked without moving her eyes from the map.

"Something older and more complex than you can fathom," the woman rustled.

"And *you* can't kill him?"

There was a softer rustling, something like a sigh.

"In your language you would call him a parasite. He is the original parasite from which all parasites come. You may also call him greed. In my language, he is my brother."

A tangled bundle of disgust, horror, and rage twisted in Hemmie's stomach. Hadn't she faced enough evil?

"Listen closely," the woman rustled after Hemmie did not speak. "Your army will attack here." She pointed to the southernmost edge of the dark spot. "But first you must gather them and wait on my word."

With that, the woman's body started to become transparent.

Hemmie reached out to her and yelled, "That's all?!?"

The woman paused, less opaque than she had been, but not yet fully transparent.

"Don't trouble yourself. Yours will not be the only army gathered for me."

The woman resumed her slow disappearance.

"Wait!" Hemmie yelled.

The woman paused again.

"I will pay my debt," she said dipping her head to show submission, "but I can't..." She shook her head. "No plantations please."

The woman pointed deeper into the swamp. "Go to Isle Dernière. Find Savary. He is a seasoned leader. You can start building my army with him."

Then, before Hemmie could wedge in another question, the woman expanded into a burst of light and disappeared.

Grand Terre Destroyed

When the woman had gone, Hemmie slowly slid down the tree. Her feet back on solid ground, the passionflower's perfume resurged, enveloping her in an explosion of sweetness. She tugged at the neck of her dress and peeked into the bodice. The passionflowers she had tucked there were crushed; their anthers leaked a sticky fluid onto her chest. The peaceful languidness she had felt before the bear attacked her had transformed into a more aggressive force. It was as if the intoxication was racing through her veins and collecting, hot and weighty, in her crotch. She started walking, mumbling, "Savary? Isle Cheneire? Isle..."

She tried to remember the name of the island she was supposed to be traveling to but the pounding in her pelvis made it hard to focus. As she walked, she found herself shortening her strides so she could press the bread bag against the fullness that was blossoming between her legs. She was contemplating grinding against a tree to get some relief, when she tripped on something underfoot. She pitched forward and slammed into a low branch. The sharp pain and the sound of moaning nearby cleared her mind. She dropped into a low squat and cowered in the leafy underbrush to hide.

The moaning continued, tapering off into a ragged gasping before surging up again. Hemmie peeked through the flora until she spied a pair of boots—toes poking upward—a few feet away. She stared at the boots' worn soles until she was sure their owner was not moving. Then she crept forward, ready to run if attacked. Above the boots was a pair of tattered pants. She moved closer to find a man lying there, half hidden in a patch of bushy-beard grass, with nothing but a bloody stump where his right hand should have been.

Hemmie stepped gingerly around his blood, which had pooled, thin and sticky, in the grass. When she leaned over the man, his eyes widened in his pale, glistening face. Death was so busy, it seemed, but it could not be bothered to pay her a visit.

"Your death has come," she said.

The man tightened his jaw, but he did not speak.

"Where are your attackers?" Hemmie looked around. It was the first time she'd said anything to a white man that was not in response to a command.

The man gritted his teeth and threw his hand over his rucksack. Hemmie was momentarily confused. That she could be a threat had not occurred to her. Her eyes fixed on his face, she grasped his sack and swiped it from underneath his hand. His hand lifted, but he was too weak to grab it back from her. Hemmie took a few steps backward and loosened the straps on the sack. The first thing she saw was his rations—a slab of salt pork and a hard biscuit. At the sight of the meat, her mouth went moist. She tossed the biscuit and pulled out her knife. She cut a slice of pork and put it into her mouth before continuing to search his sack. The meat's dry saltiness brought tears to her eyes. It had been too long since she'd had anything but bread.

The only other thing of value she found in the man's sack was his money pouch, but it was light. There were only a few coins and a small green stone. Hemmie held the stone up to the light. It glinted furiously.

"*Bos* Lafitte. Give," the man whispered.

At the name Lafitte, the instructions for Hemmie's mission came flooding back to her.

"Isle Dernière?" Hemmie asked. "Is it this way?"

"Grand Terre..." the man mumbled, "no more..."

Even Hemmie had heard of Grand Terre—Lafitte's stomping grounds where he kept his bounty and eluded the governor's warrants. She crept closer and put her hand to the man's forehead. His skin was clammy and hot to the touch. Perhaps it was the fever talking.

"Who attacked Grand Terre?" Hemmie asked.

The man closed his eyes. Another low moan escaped from his lips.

"Give," the man said without opening his eyes.

Hemmie looked at the stone in her palm, then back at the man quizzically. Here he was dying alone in a swamp and he was not begging to be saved. His dying wish was that Lafitte would know he remained loyal.

Hemmie shook his shoulder.

"Was it the British?"

He shook his head.

"Americans," he moaned.

"Americans?!"

"They took everything," the man whispered. "Shops, weapons, men. We will all..."

He trailed off without finishing his statement.

"And Isle Dernière? Did they attack all the islands?" she asked, but the man didn't reply.

Hemmie rubbed the stone with her thumb. She did not want to be pulled into the manias of this world. She didn't see what the British sniffing around the coast had to do with her. Even Governor Claiborne finally finding a way to land a blow on Lafitte had no import on her misery. She had one master now. One, she imagined, planned to keep her alive and torture her rather than allow her to slip into a peaceful final sleep.

Looking down at the dying man, she listened to the swamp shifting around her. Suddenly she could smell water. She stood and the man stared up at her through heavily lidded eyes. She needed nothing from him, but she could see from the rise and fall of his chest that death would not be swift enough to protect him from the swamp. When the animals came to feed on his flesh, he would still be alive.

The sparkling scent of the water tugged at her, but she stepped over the man and walked in the opposite direction. There had been a devil's berry bush she'd stalked past before stumbling over the dying man. She kicked her way through the underbrush, bristling at her own good will, and startled a coypu, which shot out of the overgrowth and bumped against her shins. She managed to swallow her scream, holding her breath as the fat hairy rodent waddled away.

She calmed her thrashing and moved softly through the swamp, sniffing for the devil berry's unique stink. When she found the shrub, she wrapped her hand in her skirt and reached past berries and bell-shaped blooms to rip off a handful of leaves. Dipping into her cleavage, she pulled out her medicine pouch, tucked the leaves inside, and followed her nose to the nearest creek, twisting the pouch as she went.

At the edge of the creek, she doused the pouch in the water until it was soaked all the way through. She wrapped the pouch in a huge fern leaf and retraced her steps. By the time she neared the dying man, the animals had already come. Dark furry bodies climbing over his body, nosing at his clothes, nibbling at his exposed skin. Hemmie rushed forward, clapping her hands loudly. The animals startled and streaked away, their striped tails disappearing into the surrounding underbrush.

She kneeled next to the man and pressed her wet fingers against the ground—coating them in a protective layer of dirt. Opening the pouch, she pinched a bit of devil's berry mush between her fingers, rolling it into a ball and shoving it between the dying man's lips. They were both silent as it dissolved in his mouth. Then he opened his eyes wide and gave one last moan before falling limp at Hemmie's side.

Finding Flight

In the absence of bears and dying men, Hemmie made quick time to the edge of the swamp. Death had dulled, but not destroyed, the passionflowers' spell. No longer looking longingly at trees, she was content to absentmindedly rock her hips against the bread bag as she stared out across Barataria Bay. Even after the dead man's tale, what she saw across the water was shocking. The island floating in the middle of the bay had to be Grand Terre. It was swathed in smoke. There were two smaller islands nearby looking similarly disheveled. *There is no escape from the terror*—she thought bitterly—*this is what people do: they wage war, they steal, they extinguish life.* No matter what she had lacked on her floating patch of land, it was a safer place by far than anywhere humans roamed.

A tugging at her chest pulled her toward the bay, urging her to keep moving. She scanned the shoreline, but she could see no vessels of any kind: no abandoned boats, not even a piece of flotsam large enough for her to stand on. Hemmie would have turned back, but she knew that if she did not obey, the tugging would become more insistent—even dunk her in the bay if that was the only way to get her across the water.

When she spun around to walk the shore, she was startled by a cluster of color hanging in midair. She stumbled backward. Suddenly a hummingbird peeled away from the crush, darting near to dip toward her chest. Watching it bob around her breasts, Hemmie remembered the passionflowers that had been crushed against her chest. The mesmerizing blur of the hummingbird's wings sparked an idea. She unclasped her capelet and shoved it into her food pouch. Unbuttoning the top of her dress, she untied the neck of her slip and laid her shoulders and chest bare. Without hesitation, the hummingbirds swooped in, pressing their tiny beaks against her body to sip sweetness from the wells of her skin.

As the birds were drinking their fill, Hemmie slowly spread her arms and began humming. Her song wafted through the air, drawing the hummingbirds away from their drinking to perch on her outstretched arms. Her face broke into a wide grin, then she calmed herself and willed the hummingbirds to fly. Without hesitation, they took flight, gracefully lifting off the ground, carrying a squealing Hemmie high into the air.

The hummingbirds carried Hemmie soaring over Barataria Bay, drifting past the burning islands of Grand Terre, Grande Isle, and Cheniere Caminda. At the sandy shores of Isle Dernière, they dipped, lowering Hemmie down as softly as if she weighed no more than a feather. Tottering in the sand, she stopped humming and waited for the hummingbirds to flit away. Adjusting her dress, she trudged across the sand, following the tugging sensation inland to where the sand gave way to foliage.

Entering the forest, she realized the hummingbirds had not left, instead they clouded behind her head as if awaiting their reward. She put her hands on her hips, primed to tell them not to be greedy, but before she could speak, her leg started throbbing, reminding her that she could not fly. She had stolen the power of flight from them.

She walked deeper into the wild green of the island's forest, rolling her fingers over her chest as she went. The remaining passionflower petals peeled off her skin and crushed together, forming a tight ball. Hemmie dug a hole in the grass with the toe of her boot, dropped the ball of flower petals inside, covered it with dirt, and lifted her skirts. Her reconstructed leg ached, but she ignored it to squat over the buried flowers. Her urine drenched the earth. With the release, a stream of delight filtered through her. Against her own instinct, she couldn't help but marvel at how far she'd come. It was a marvel that—since she'd landed back in the swamps—she had managed to evade a bear, help a dying man, and entice a charm of hummingbirds to help her fly across a bay.

She dropped her skirts, stepped away from the planting, and watched as a green bud pushed out of the dirt, snaking across the grass to unfurl into a full-grown passionflower vine. Scooping it up, she draped it over a hairyfruit chervil bush and asked, "Will that do?" So busy were they, swarming the flowers and flitting into buds, the hummingbirds gave no reply.

Finally, a Release

Hemmie's shins burned, the hems of her underskirts were full of burrs, and her throat was dry. The forest was all a carpet of pennywort and random eruptions of tall twisted trees with no obvious footpaths or clearings. The tugging had abandoned her, leaving her to stumble through the green for over an hour. To confuse her even further, the newly sprouted passionflower blooms had flooded her with carnal intoxication all over again. Hemmie opened her flask, gulped down a mouthful of rum, and leaned against a tree. The scent of passionflower pounded through her like a drum.

A low, grating sound behind her caused her to tense; she didn't have the energy to flee. Peering around the tree, she saw that there was no danger—only a deer digging through leaves in the center of a stand of trees. The deer heard Hemmie's rustling and its head darted up, alert and still. For a few seconds neither Hemmie nor the deer moved. The fading light of the sun bathed them both in a soft glow.

The deer crept forward to sniff at Hemmie's wrists. Intrigued, Hemmie reached out and stroked its neck. Warmth and softness shocked the cells in Hemmie's palm. The deer raised its head and nosed at Hemmie's waist and breasts. She gasped. The deer jerked its head away, startled at the sound. Hemmie caught her breath and skirted around to the opposite side of the tree. She gripped the tree trunk, great gusts of arousal swirling through her. The deer followed, standing at her side to stare at her quizzically. Hemmie drew in a sharp breath, and turned her face away.

Her cheek pressed against tree bark and her eyes squeezed shut, Hemmie felt a nuzzle at her armpit, then something collide with her thighs. She opened her eyes in time to see the deer flick its tail, showing a flash of white. Then it backed up against her, causing an explosion within. Sensation broke over her like a sudden thunderstorm. She gave in and reached for the deer, grasping its flanks, thrusting hesitantly at first, then pushing harder, reaching toward her arousal, urging it to swell larger and larger until it consumed her. Pleasure compressed and she was struck by a few intense blows before multiple waves washed through her, shaking her body from her scalp to the soles of her feet.

Her limbs went slack. She loosened her grip on the deer and leaned against the tree trunk. While she waited for the thudding of her heart to subside, the deer skittered away. For a few blissful seconds, she was delivered from everything but the uncontrollable aftershocks of her encounter. When her body had ceased its shuddering, she pulled out her flask and drank deeply. By the time she'd returned the cap to the flask, the details of her mission came flooding back in. The forest was as impenetrable and mysterious as it had been when she had begun, but she pushed herself off the tree, shook out her skirts, and resumed her stumbling through the greenery. She knew the watery-ness of her movements was due to the intervention of the gleaming woman, but she shook off the thought. Perhaps there would be time to figure out what the apparition had done to her. For now, she recommitted to the task at hand and focused on finding her way out of the forest.

The Search for Savary

When Hemmie finally found the town at the heart of the island, there were no signs of an invading army and nothing had been set ablaze, yet the town looked battered and vacant. In the town square, a cadre of boys stood in a loose circle joking with each other in raspy, war-weary voices. As Hemmie approached, they snapped to attention, closing ranks so that their bodies formed a barrier.

Hemmie grabbed her food pouch and the boys reached into their waistbands and drew swords. Swords?

She laughed.

"Your commander doesn't trust you with guns?"

She slowly untied the pouch from her waist, lowered it to the ground.

"You boys look hungry," she said and laid the pouch open.

The boy's eyes widened when they saw the food. Hemmie picked up two chunks of bread and held them out. One of the boys pitched forward, reaching for the bread. Another boy slapped his hand and pulled him back. Hemmie dropped the bread and held up her hands as if her empty palms proved her innocence.

"Look, I mean you no harm," she said. "I just baked it this morning."

The boys edged nearer, but no one broke ranks until the tall boy in the middle stepped forward and grabbed a chunk of bread from the pile at Hemmie's feet. Then they all swarmed, swiping pieces of bread until the sack was completely empty. Watched them gobble the bread, hands pushing against mouths, Hemmie became aware of her own hunger. Her stomach growled.

She backed away from the boys and turned her back to slide the salt pork out from its hiding place. She quickly sliced the pork into two thick slabs, tucked them into a hunk of bread she'd saved for herself. In privacy, she devoured the sandwich, listening as the boys drifted off into conversation. When their words lost their tense edges, she wiped her mouth and approached them again.

"I need to see Savary."

"He's not going to see you," the leader said, crossing his arms.

"It's important." Hemmie tensed her jaw and tried to compel him to let her pass, but he just shook his head and tightened his hand on his sword.

Hemmie started clearing her throat hoping the friction would trigger the mist that had sent the bear away, but the air refused to shift at her command. As she was contemplating slinking away in defeat, she noticed one of the boys looking directly at her while the others threw passing glances in her direction and avoided her gaze.

With a slight nod to the leader, she turned away, slowly walking back the way she came. When she was almost out of sight, she dropped a piece of bread on the ground and hid behind a decrepit shed near the edge of the forest. The boys resumed their milling about, but the watchful one snuck over and scooped up the bread. Hemmie lunged out of her hiding place, grabbed him by the arm, and dragged him behind the shed.

"Take me to Savary!" she said and fixed the boy with a fierce glare.

The boy fidgeted, but he did not speak.

"Did they capture him with Lafitte?"

The boy bucked his body, struggling to shake Hemmie off, but she held tight.

"He's not here," the boy said, slouching when he saw that he could not break Hemmie's hold.

"Where is he?"

"Fighting the British."

"With the Americans?"

"The governor made him a major," the boy said, his voice swelling with pride.

Hemmie dropped the boy's arm.

"Where is this battle?"

The boy shrugged. He didn't flee but he kept his eye on her as he devoured the bread.

"Fighting the British," she mumbled to herself. She crossed her arms and began to pace. It was foolish to wander into war. Surely the glimmering woman didn't rebuild muscle and bone for Hemmie to end up more mangled than she began. Then she remembered the woman's words. She wanted a battalion—the men were what she was after. Hemmie whirled around to face the boy.

"How many men did he take with him?"

The boy jumped as if startled by her question. Then he stared at her as if measuring her intent. His frame was slight, but his eyes were hard as if he'd already seen battle.

"All of the men are gone." He lifted his chest proudly. "He left us to protect the island."

Hemmie fished around in her pocket and found a small corner of salt pork. She handed it to the boy in silence and stalked away. Stomping into the forest, she had nothing but failure on her mind. She stopped short. Retracing her steps, cutting a path back to shore, was pointless. She was a woman completely adrift. Even if she could find her way back to the exact stretch of swamp over which her magical patch of land had hovered, she had no way to get back up there. She had been housed by her predators, and then by her savior. She had no map, no home, no secrets of return. Everything she possessed was strapped to her: the traveling dress, a few petticoats, the empty medicine pouch, the rifle, the knife, a few sips of rum, a dry rind of salt pork, and the breadcrumbs lining the bottom of her food sack. Now she would have to find shelter on her own.

She turned back, planning to find a place among the boys. She'd help them grow food to nourish their skinny frames, she thought, *until*—she held the word heavy and round in her mind— until the woman came for her. Just that quickly—as soon as she had begun to formulate a plan—she felt something new. She felt that she could make choices and establish something to call her own. She was choosing her own direction, as if her hands, her skin, her bones were her own.

The moment she stepped out of the forest, her imaginings of what she could be were taking away from her. There was a heat growing in her palms. She held her hands in front of her face and saw a pale mist rising from them.

"No," she yelled, and pushed her hands into her pockets.

She wanted a few more seconds to relish the sensation that she was on her own. She wanted to hold on to that glimmer of what it meant to be her own person. But she did not belong to herself. Hiding her hands in her pockets did nothing to stop the mist from seeping from her hands and leaking into the air.

By the time she made it back to the town square, the mist had overwhelmed her. When she was completely shrouded in thick fog, she was forced to yank her hands from her pockets and flail them around to disperse the mist. As her arms arced through the air, she noticed that her palms left behind thick streaks of mist that seemed more solid than the cloudiness clogging the air. When she had outrun the mist, she reached out and plucked one of the solid streaks. It vibrated at her touch, curling like a tendril of hair. Curious, she ran her fingers along its length. Under the pressure of her fingertips, it stretched into a long strand. Pulling the strand into playful shapes, she was drenched in a musky, pungent odor. She sniffed her hands, then the strands of mist. Everything smelled of field workers drenched in sweat at day's end. She remembered how the funk of their efforts left a palpable cloud lingering long after they had trudged past.

A smile grabbed hold of her lips. These scents had to belong to Savary's men. Driven by some mix of instinct or intuition, she rushed around, collecting the strands of scent. She stretched them into long lengths before weaving them into fat strands that, when joined, began to whip back and forth, straining toward the swamp.

The urgent reaching of the woven strands spurred Hemmie into action. She emptied the air of the men's musk, creating a long coil of rope made of the woven mist. Then she started to sculpt. There was no commanding tugging bossing her about, no maddening puppetry forcing her into action. The urge to work the strands into a broad, muscular body came from Hemmie's imagination. The inspiration for the four strong legs she built beneath the body was hers alone.

When her work was complete, she stood back, overcome with pride. She admired the steed; it was strong and steady, crafted completely from the scents left behind by Savary's army. In an instant, she choked down her excitement. Hauling herself up onto the steed's back, she pulled out her flask and drained it. 'You have no cause for celebration,' she chided herself. "You are still a puppet who will never know the taste of freedom.' She grabbed two fists full of the horse's mane as it cantered, shifting and jittery, beneath her weight. She tightened her thighs around its sides, leaned forward, and whispered, "Go." Then she held on tight as the steed streaked forward to hurtle across the sky.

The Darkness Revealed

The horse barreled over the swamp with long, gliding leaps. Hemmie felt as if she was holding on to a comet. After hiding her face against the horse's neck, she risked a peek down at the landscape as it whisked by below. Off the coast of Barataria, the gulf was clogged with ships—hundreds of them, their decks teeming with cannons and soldiers. The swamp left behind, they sped over plantations, flashing past the bent backs of cane cutters hunched over in the interminable rows of sugarcane. She caught the glint of machetes as they arced up and fell down, separating plant from earth. Past the plantations, they reached New Orleans, racing over its huge wooden gates and dilapidated forts. As they galloped ahead, an eerie coolness drifted up from the city. Its streets were empty, its gutters were overflowing of sewage, and corrals of horses filled the city's courtyards. There were soldiers everywhere, manning the moat, guarding blockades, but the city did not feel secure. There was something dark and chilling below. Suddenly an invisible weight hooked into their bodies and dragged them downward. Struggling to keep the steed aloft, Hemmie frantically searched the city streets, looking for whatever force was trying to abort their flight.

As her panic intensified, the city opened to her. The barriers of walls and roofs peeled away, and she could see humans of every height and shade inside the city's homes: French ship owners, Acadian traders, German merchants, Choctaw hunters, Castillian soldiers, American-born lawyers, all moving around in secret as they plotted with generals and housed militia in preparation for impending war. She looked even closer and saw in the shadows, her people—people whose bodies had been scarred, mutilated, and mangled. They toiled in kitchens, basements, nurseries, and stables despite having been turned inside out, their realities ruptured and violence forced upon them as the language of their lives.

Soon the horse slid low enough for its hooves to strike rooftops. Hemmie dug in and gritted her teeth, pushing her heels against the horse's sides to urge it onward and upward. When the horse dipped even lower, Hemmie saw a sickening sight. Whether free or enslaved, all the people of New Orleans had a thin black cord wrapped around their necks. The cords ran toward the center of the city, tangling in denser and denser clumps. Hemmie yanked at the horse's mane desperate to flee.

The horse carried them gliding over the city's main plaza. There, under the watchful presence of the Cabildo, a bulging, bulbous blob sat, occupying the heart of the city. Everything about it—its bruise-colored skin, its massive size, its undulating pulsing—filled Hemmie with dread. In distinct opposition to the glimmering apparition who had saved Hemmie, the blob absorbed all light, consuming any energy and activity in its vicinity. Before they could streak by, the blob extended a dark, sticky cord into the sky. Despite its upward stretching, the horse strained ahead, speeding past to escape the lazy lick of the cord.

By the time they left the city, Hemmie was clammy and shaken. The horse was unaffected. It did not slow its gallop toward the sources of its scent. Soon they were flying over a battlefield full of weary men. Hemmie stared into the melee, trying to make sense of the battle. She identified red-coated men and blue-coated men, but they seemed to mete out pain indiscriminately, swarming over each other with no sense of order or strategy. All of their uniforms were torn and bloodied, and each soldier seemed to be lunging at anyone within striking distance. As soon as they had passed the battle, the horse plunged downward. Hemmie held on tightly as the steed thudded down to the earth, striking the dirt with its mighty hooves.

When they were finally galloping over the land, Hemmie exhaled. The horse slowed its long swift strides at a small lively camp. It pranced through the camp, circulating around groups of men that were scattered about. No matter what the men were doing—keeping warm by the fire, eating from tin plates, sharpening knives, talking—they all looked up in glassy-eyed shock to see Hemmie riding a ropy steed made of mist. At the center of the camp, in front of a large tent, the horse came to a halt.

Hemmie slid to the ground and reached up to pat the steed in thanks, but her fingers touched nothing but air. The horse had already dissolved, each scent unfurling and flying off toward its source to rejoin the skin from which it sprang.

Savary, At Last

Hemmie stood frozen in front of the tent. She had worked so hard to find him, but she had not considered what she would say when she arrived.

"Have you come for work?" The voice came from within the tent.

Hemmie peeked into the slit at the tent's opening. Inside she saw a man sitting at a rough wood table at the back of the tent. He had dark skin and a scar splitting his left cheek. Hemmie noted the teacup and saucer at his elbow, the cluster of disassembled guns littering the table.

"We are in need of nurses," Savary said when Hemmie could not find her words.

He picked up the muzzle of one of his guns and began to polish it.

"From the activities of your men, it seems that you are more in need of a battle," Hemmie said, stepping into the tent.

Savary looked up at her, spearing her with an intense squint.

"Anyone working for the British will be shot immediately."

Hemmie shook her head mutely.

"I know the offer they made Lafitte," he continued looking back down at his gun. "They won't find any spies or turncoats here. I'm loyal to the French."

Hemmie scrunched her face in confusion.

"The French?" she asked. Whether it was the French, the

Spanish, or perhaps soon—the British—whoever ruled the city, her fortunes had never changed. How this wild-haired man, with skin dark as hers could imagine his allegiances could alter his life was unfathomable to her.

"Is it not Governor Claiborne you represent? And the French, they have long since lost their battles. Where are they now, while your battalion is lounging around with no enemy to fight?"

Savary was silent as he continued rubbing a dirty rag against the muzzle he was cleaning. He looked up at her, eyes glinting. "You have not stated your allegiance."

"Allegiance?" Hemmie laughed. The force she represented barely had her comprehension, let alone her allegiance. Her mind raced through the memory of what she had seen: knew what she had seen: the glimmering woman who had altered Hemmie's future; the bruise-colored blob pulsing in the heart of the city; her own mangled limb made anew. She could not fathom the words she could use to explain any of this to Savary. The conversation would unravel the moment she told him the truth of her mission.

"I'm an experienced nurse," she said, stalling for time. "I can serve your army well. How often should I expect the battalion to fight?" She asked, taking a step toward him. "How many times has the company been to battle?"

"Once, but we are expecting major casualties on our next front."

"While you are preparing for the next battle, are you sure the Governor is not fighting the major battles without you? Leaving you sitting here while other battalions are out winning the war?"

One side of Savary's mouth creased.

"The activities of this battalion will not be managed by a nurse. Have you ever served during war?"

Hemmie thought of all the mangled bodies she'd helped bandage, all the fevers she'd helped break; the accidents with the machines, with fire, the beatings, the missing limbs, the childbirth.

"This is not war," she said. "I can lead you to war."

Savary slammed the muzzle down on the tabletop and charged at Hemmie. He grabbed her by the arm.

"Who are you spying for?"

"No one, no one," she sputtered.

Savary searched her face.

"I saw the British in battle as I was headed here and I thought..."

"You're a runaway," he said and he turned her loose. "I don't harbor fugitives."

Hemmie laughed.

"Fugitive?!? And what are you?"

"You are speaking to the commander of the Second Battalion of the Louisiana Militia, and a second major in the U.S. Army," Savary boomed. "I earned my place in this army and I will be fighting alongside the other commanders until the blood of the British darkens these shores."

Hemmie's eyes hardened. This was a fool's errand. This man would not follow anyone but the French. They had him under a spell that was as unbreakable as the one that had dragged her across the swamp.

"And what then?" she asked. "You think your fighting will make you welcome in their society? Even if you succeed, you think the city will throw roses at your feet?"

Savary sat back down and picked up a firing lock.

"You may go now," he said softly.

Hemmie clenched her fists. She imagined the glimmering woman hovering in air overhead, crackling with disappointment. She looked down at her hands, expecting them to mist, but they were cold and bare. She took a deep breath and stepped even closer to Savary.

"I have been sent to tell you there is a supernatural battle being fought that will determine the future of this city just as sure as this flesh and blood battle with the British will." She started rubbing her hands together to heat them. "Abandon this farce. They will use you to fight and toss you away when the war is won. I will show you where you are truly needed."

When she had built a heat in her hands, she spread her fingers in front of Savary's face. Savary stared at her, tense and waiting, but nothing happened. There was no mist, no shower of sparks, no glowing maps of the city.

"You are mad!" he yelled after Hemmie had stood there unmoving, holding her palms up as if they were weapons. He grabbed her by the elbow and dragged her to the entrance of his tent.

"Enjoy your title," she yelled as he steered her out. "You'll be a fugitive just as soon as they don't need you. Help them win their victories and you are helping them keep you their prey...."

Savary rolled the flap closed before Hemmie could finish her rant. She stood in front of the tent, muttering under her breath; then she stalked away, patting her hands over her body to check her pouches, weapons, and provisions. The pouches were empty, the provisions had been eaten; the weapons were the only useful thing left to her.

At the edge of the camp, she peeked into the forest on one side, then walked a few paces to peer into the greenery again. No patch of forest seemed to hold any promise or portent. She imagined herself letting go—releasing every bit of effort that kept her on her feet and melting to the ground in a quiet, defeated heap.

"Need a horse?"

Hemmie looked up to see one of Savary's soldiers leaning

against his horse. His muscular limbs were relaxed, but his smirk suggested that he would be ready to laugh or attack at the slightest provocation. Something about him sparked a bit of hope in Hemmie. She drew herself up tall.

"I need an army."

The man laughed and stepped into the stirrups. Hemmie watched the graceful arc of his leg as he threw it over the horse's width. He settled into the saddle, then leaned down to offer his hand to her.

"If it's an army you need, I'll help you build it."

Hemmie searched for a shimmer around his unkempt hair, but all she saw was the sparkling burning in his eyes.

"Ride," the woman rustled in her mind.

"But I failed," Hemmie said aloud.

Rustling exploded in Hemmie's ears, loud and layered. The sound slithered over and around, amplifying itself with every twist and turn. Hemmie clamped her hands over her ears.

"You have not failed. You have exceeded my expectations."

"I don't..."

"I don't want Savary, he's not up to the task. I already have a commander for my army," the woman rustled.

Hemmie dropped her hands from her ears and looked up at the man on the horse. He smiled down at her.

"You," the rustling boomed in her mind. "You are my commander. I hope this exercise has cleared your mind."

Hemmie froze, her mind stumbling to decode the woman's meaning, to make sense of the journey that had led her here.

"We have a long battle ahead of us—one that won't be won in this century, and possibly not the next. I need someone unbreakable. Have you cleared away all that was poisoning you?"

Hemmie put her hand to her pocket and squeezed the flask that was hidden there. She had not missed the alcohol, even now that it had run dry. She had no urge to shrink away from the man towering over her on horseback and she had not been afraid of Savary. Somehow—as she had tasted flight twice and surrendered to waves of pleasure—she had lost her throbbing pain, her manic need to hide, her deep desire for death.

"Do you believe in our mission?"

Hemmie thought of the sickening lump in the middle of the city, its dark cords siphoning energy from everyone in its radius.

She nodded.

"Good," the woman rustled. "*I have gathered your army. It's time to ride.*"

Hemmie checked that her rifle was secure, then grasped the soldier's hand. She swung herself up, mounted the horse, and gripped his waist. On her word, he kicked the horse into motion. Their bodies jerked backward as the animal surged into action. Then, as if they were one being, they pitched themselves forward, lowering their heads out of the wind to race unhindered toward Hemmie's destiny.

Note: Joseph Savary, a native of Saint-Dominique (Haiti), fought with the French during the Haitian Revolution. When Haiti became independent, Savary and his family settled in Barataria, Louisiana, home of Pierre and Jean Lafitte, notorious pirates who operated off the coast of Louisiana and Spanish Texas. Savary single-handedly raised his 256-member Second Battalion, Free Men of Color of the Louisiana Militia and was inducted into service on December 19, 1814. After fighting back the British on the banks of the Mississippi River, the Second Battalion and other all-black battalions were held in reserve during the main Battle of New Orleans on January 8, 1815. Savary's battalion defied orders and rushed to the front. Savary's men killed British Commanding General Pakenham on the field of battle. At the end of the conflict Jackson publicly praised the Second Battalion and its commander. When the war ended, however, Jackson, at the request of New Orleans's white residents who feared a slave uprising, ordered all black troops out of the city. Savary returned to Spanish Texas where he was welcomed by Pierre Lafitte. He eventually moved to New Orleans in 1822, after joining Mexican rebels fighting for their nation's independence. The adventures of Hemmie the Swamp Witch have been lost to history.

VOLCANO WOMAN

He creeps up on me, quiet-like. A funky whisky scent invades me. "Hey, cutie."

He stands close. His scabs and scars make my skin crawl. When I take a step back, he scowls.

"Why you actin scared, I jus wan talk to you. Maybe take you to a hotel."

One jittery look around shows me empty lots and boarded-up buildings. Even the street is dead: no traffic. I glance at him out the corner of my eye, then I step off the curb and scoot across the street real quick.

The slap of my shoes is loud on the concrete, but I can hear the beat of his feet coming after me. Next thing I know, my knee twists and I'm tumbling. From the ground, I see him gaining on me. I scramble sideways, scraping my palms as I work my way underneath a chain-link fence.

Inside, all I see is rows and rows of hanging car parts. I duck tire rims and rusty engines, limping through the mess of metal to find a place to hide.

I hunch down behind a curtain of dusty license plates, but I am not alone.

"Girlie, you all right?"

I whirl around to see an old woman sitting on a throne of twisted car fenders. Thick, gray strands of hair are coiled high on her head. I nod mutely, keeping my eyes on two huge dogs sprawled at her feet.

"Soup?" she says, and motions to a huge pot billowing steam.

I shake my head "no" and look back toward the street.

"Girl, you come to my yard with a wolf chasin you and you in a rush to go back into the night?"

In a flash, she is standing, her arm outstretched, holding a warm cup of soup. My hand lifts to take the soup. I try to lower my arm, but it's no use: my body is not under my control.

The soup makes me dizzy and limp. I drop down to the dirt and lay there paralyzed while the old woman trickles a ragged line of salt in a circle around my body.

"What do you see?" she whispers.

My eyes slip closed, and I see a figure dancing around the rim of a volcano.

"Go."

At her command, I walk toward four clay pots at the base of the volcano. The dancing figure descends, striding down the volcano in two big steps. We mirror each other, standing on either side of the pots.

"Clean yourself."

The dancing figure undresses me. When I am nude, I dip my hands into the first pot. Black paste coats my fingers.

"Roach dung," she whispers, and I slather it on my body.

I dig into the next pot, scooping up rotten fruit to work into my hair. Tree sap from the third pot cakes my armpits. The gin from the last pot splatters my skin.

"Now stand."

I rise and the dancing figure rises with me. Before my eyes, she glows brighter and brighter. Suddenly, she bursts into flame.

I back away, but the sparks shooting from her body pierce my skin and fill me with fury. My eyes roll back in my head and every muscle in my body starts trembling. Then, without warning, my cells split open and I erupt.

When I wake, my body is stiff and cold. The old woman is leaning over me.

"Go home, baby."

I sit up and brush dirt off the side of my face.

"Don't talk to nobody, don't look at nobody. Go straight home."

I am sluggish. My head hurts and the woman's voice sounds far away. Old bony fingers grab my arm and drag me to my feet.

"Go now," she says. "Go."

I stagger into the street, lurching toward home. Car tires screech around me. The stench of liquor worms into my nostrils.

"Been looking for you, baby."

The volcano woman stirs. I feel her sparks tickling my throat.

The man grabs my wrist.

"Leave me...the fuck...alone," I growl and the volcano woman explodes. I look at him, light shooting from my eyes. I sink my heat into his flesh, finding fuel in the pitch of his screeching. I feel as if I am aflame. He jerks, then falls, trembling and gasping at my feet.

I turn away from the onlookers and race home. I walk up the stairs, my limbs tingling and my palms wet. The heat is still bubbling under my skin. My keys slip against my sweat as I wrestle the lock open and slam the door behind me. I slide to the floor, panting with deep savage breaths.

"You're safe," the volcano woman flutters.

She spins with her arms flung wide. Her spirals whip up a cocoon of warm winds. I fling my limbs wide and let her rage wash me clean.

BECAUSE OF THE BONE MAN

The First Surge

The rocks loved the touch of air on their sharp points. With the season of wet winds past and the mugginess swept away, the air was full of a delicious coolness that the rocks loved to bathe in. But a man—long and gangly—had draped himself over them, pressing his limbs into their gaps. They hated his weight and the oblivious way he smothered them in his slumber, clogging the soothing emptiness that surrounded them.

It was difficult to wake him, but if they really tried, they could do it. They had to harden their edges, focus on their points, and push as hard as they could against his bones. That he was bony was a thing the rocks knew. When they woke him, poking at his layers of skin and muscle, he would break contact and rise up from among them. Then the blessed breeze would be free to brush against their hard, grainy facets again and again.

Each time the man woke, he would stand on the rocks' uneven surfaces and stare into the dark, murky waters of the canal. When he was still like that—his face blank, his jaw hard—he seemed as if he were one of them: sturdy, unmoving, timeless. But the stillness would always end. He would turn his back to the canal and push off the rocks, scrambling upward until he reached the top of the levee. Then there was nothing more for the rocks to know. They would never roll up to the top of the levee and gaze at the land on the other side. They would never know that—as the man stood atop the levee, staring at the land on the dry side of the levee—there was nothing to see but rubble.

Whenever the man sighed, the rocks felt a barely perceptible ripple in air around them. They did not know that the rippling air came from the sudden shock of pain that pierced him each time he laid his eyes on the sea of debris that seemed to stretch on forever. The rocks did not know pain, but they knew silence. They knew absence. They knew the moment the man slipped away from them, pitching himself into a run down the grass that covered the dry side of the levee. His feet tensed to stop him from tumbling, he chanted to protect himself from the deep hollows of silence that lay before him.

"Let's go get 'em. Let's go get 'em."

He repeated the chant over and over, imagining a ghostly syncopation of foot stomps and tambourine slaps rounding out the whisper of his words. Every morning the destruction washed over him as if it were a new thing, and every morning he beat back the panic by holding on to the chant's intonations.

Sometimes the chant could not soothe him. On these days, no matter how forcefully he chanted, he couldn't dam up the memories that lapped at his brain. On those days, speeding down the levee was the same as somersaulting backward in time. He was surrounded by the chaos all over again. The winds and rains pounding his father's house, the churning waters spilling over from swollen waterways to break levees and pummel houses in their rush through neighborhoods. Now that the structures had been soaked and knocked off their foundations, he was trapped in this demolished landscape.

Trying to ignore the sound his sanity was making as it slipped from his grasp was a daily, desperate task. The city was his oxygen and he was its heartbeat. He believed in its seasons and its rituals. To see it lying in shambles, gutted like a catfish, was a horror his mind could not assimilate. He knew there was only one way to rebuild, one force that could jolt the city back into functioning, back to its parade of decrepit ways. The only thing to be done was to carry on.

Were it not for the bridge, he would be carrying on. He was the Bone Man and he had to set the city in motion. He needed to gather the noise makers and the bone shakers for their annual ramble through town, but each time he tried to set a course for home, the bridge thwarted him. It loomed over the destruction like a skeletal specter rising in air. A sprawl of long concrete ramps and a corroded steel frame, the bridge connected the ghostland where the Bone Man was trapped to the rest of the city.

On this day, as on all days, he mounted the bridge. His pouch was weighty with found treasure that he hoped would gain him entry across the bridge. His feet were heavy as he strode up the concrete ramp. The pouch bouncing against his leg carried a photograph with a splintered frame, the image marred by a chemical splotches, blooming indigo and magenta across a family's faces; a stiff, wrinkled envelope stuffed with a hand-written letter whose words had become illegible; and a bone-white plastic recorder, its mouthpiece smashed and jagged-edged. He began the chant again, focusing on the objects in his pouch instead of his prospects for success.

He stepped onto the metal grate and held his breath. Before he could take another step, the barrier—a curtain of glittering lights—materialized from thin air. He squinted in the harsh glare of the lights, tensing against the images the curtain reflected. He was doused in the curtain's yellow glow as wavering images of the city undulated across the curtain's surface. The curtain revealed giggling white couples on Magazine Street as they sat at sidewalk cafes, drank coffee, and popped in and out of stores. It projected a partially reconstructed house swarming with a construction crew on Bayou St. John. Standing there with the lights reflecting yellow on his skin, the Bone Man had seen the city limping back into shape, progressing from paralysis to activity. His impotence was always sharp and raging as he witnessed the cityscapes he could not enter, but he found himself trembling in anger as the curtain shifted to show him a large ballroom filled with white women in gowns and white men in tuxedos. The crowd erupted into applause.

"I'm running out of time," he muttered as he watched the coronation of an opulently dressed Mardi Gras king and queen.

Desperation surged. He grabbed the objects out of his pouch and hurled them at the sparkling lights. But the curtain was unmoved. The objects bounced off the lights, one by one, and went slamming into the bridge's metal grate. The objects were destroyed, but the image of the couples persisted, and they carried on with their Carnival pageantry undisturbed.

The Bone Man clenched his fists and stepped forward. His home was on the other side. His crew—if any of them were left—was on the other side. The work he had sworn to do—to keep the city's magic churning—had to be done on the other side of the bridge.

"Stay back," a chorus of voices hissed as he neared the curtain. "You have nothing we need." He had never heard the voices before. They reached out toward him as if they were just behind the curtain of light.

"I need to go home," he yelled. The voices went silent. When the Bone Man saw the glittering of the curtain go still, he threw his arms over his face and ran forward. Upon his touch, the curtain compressed itself into sharp spikes. As he went crashing into them, they surged upward, shoving him backward onto the concrete ramp. A hoarse cry fell from his lips and he tumbled to the ground. A burning sensation flared across his palms and his side throbbed. He crawled to his hands and knees, then slowly climbed to his feet. The curtain was calm again, its lights smoothed back into a serene, shimmering surface. The Bone Man scooped up the shards of shattered treasure, stuffed them into his bag, and—ignoring the curtain's reflection of the world he longed to return to—limped back to the destruction below.

He returned to the rambling spread of destruction, reading the wreckage by its markers: a parade of empty concrete stairs that dotted the debris, relics of a time before the storm when the land held neat rows of homes—shotgun structures, camelbacks too—houses that had held all manner of wonderful, troubled, fascinating, fulfilling life. Now these concrete stumps led nowhere and held nothing but air.

He had the habit of ignoring the concrete steps. They got under his skin. With their unyielding presence, they felt like some inanimate version of himself. Like him, they had been rendered mute, nothing more than footprints, unmoving pieces of proof that before roofs collapsed and walls shattered there was a home here, and there, and a few more over there.

On this day, for the first time, as he waded through the wreckage, kicking aside wood slats, rusty nails, and soggy insulation, he spied a set of concrete stairs that was not empty. He struggled past everything splintered and waterlogged in his path to get a closer look. There was something golden and glinting beckoning him. When nearer the stairs, he saw a gold pendant on top the stairs' flat concrete platform. He rested his foot on the bottom stair and paused. Wild imaginings of the people who lived there burst into his mind. Had they been happy? Did they love the city as much as he did? Were they able to breathe now that they had been swept away by the storm, or trapped in a festering shelter, or exiled in some far-flung state? Against his will, an itch to hold the pendant flared across his palms. He mounted the stairs, pushing through the feeling that he was walking across a grave. As he climbed, each step felt as if he were leaving his footprints on something sacred.

On the top step, an invisible wall forced him to stop short. Incomprehension, then rage surged up in him. What if the pendant was the thing that could part the curtain on the bridge? He pounded at the air, both hands balled into fists, but—as if the air had solidified—his fists banged against a smooth flexible surface that bent slightly at his touch. He banged harder and was shocked into stillness when a flash of light erupted. The light sizzled into the shape of a house. Within the blazing structure, the Bone Man was stunned to discover—where the weight of a house once rested—was the slight body of a child.

He tensed his muscles and gave a mighty shove against the ghostly house. With a pop, the walls gave way, and—at the same instant—the child snapped awake. When the child looked around, his face slack with sleep, he saw that he was sitting on a tiny island of concrete surrounded by debris as far as the eye could see. The child's face tightened and his eyes widened, then his eyelids began a rapid fluttering as if he were being flooded with memories. The pendant forgotten, the Bone Man kneeled next to the child. He could not stop the horror of reality from slowly filtering in. The flattened houses, collapsed roofs, and battered trees—none of it could be erased and for anyone marooned here, none of it could be ignored.

Before he could reach out to the child, the Bone Man felt a few droplets of water splatter his shoulder. He looked up expecting dark clouds; instead he saw a flat, undulating patch of murky water hovering overhead. The Bone Man stared up at it, his mind scrambling to make sense of what he was seeing. The patch of water swooped closer, and suddenly, the Bone Man could see a clear, crisp image in the rippling water.

The Bone Man found himself frozen in place, looking right into the wide eyes of a young boy. The child on the platform next to him began to wail. The Bone Man felt the crying child's growing hysteria, but he could not look away from the hovering patch of water. The boy peeking out at him was standing in an attic, staring out through a small window. The boy's house was surrounded by intact structures, and, on the roof above his head, a man and a woman waved desperately into the blue sky. The boy was still, staring at the Bone Man blankly while stuffing his fist into his mouth.

The Bone Man stood. He wanted to soothe the mania flickering in the boy's eyes. He wanted to calm him so that there was no need for the boy to gnaw at his knuckles. The cries of the child next to him were sharpening into wild howls, but the Bone Man could not turn to tend to him. The boy in the attic was unraveling. His expression—growing tighter and tighter—radiated awareness, as if he knew death was coming, just as soon as the floodwaters rose high enough to drown him.

When the patch of water floated even closer, the boy slowly reached out. The Bone Man lifted his hand to clasp the boy's, but the boy was not reaching for him. Instead the boy grasped a rope that ran out of the window into the floodwaters and tugged at it. Before the Bone Man could make out what the rope was tied to, a deluge of water crashed onto the concrete platform. The Bone Man hunched his shoulders and covered his head as the water slammed into his scalp and pounded his skin. His eyes squeezed tight, the Bone Man had a sudden flash of clarity. Attached to the rope was a corpse that floated just outside the attic window. In a cascade of images, the Bone Man saw everything: the rope tied around the corpse's waist, the dead hands frozen in rigor mortis, a dark blue skirt fanning out around the corpse's stiff body.

The downpour of water changed direction without warning. In its rush upward, the water punched him underneath his jaw and battered his bones. He frantically wiped his face, but there was nothing more to see. Once again, the platform was empty. The Bone Man snapped his head upwards and saw that as the floating patch glided away, there was a tiny pair of feet protruding from beneath its murky layers. The patch of water rose high into the sky until it disappeared. The Bone Man had lost both the child on the platform and the child in the water, and his isolation was sharper than ever.

The rocks had come to think of evening as the time the man was among them. It was not known whether he would return from the wreckage silent or sighing, growling or crying, but they knew that when they felt his weight after a long absence, the next sensation would be the cling of plastic as he spread it over their points. Then they would feel the thump of things thudding against their surfaces as he emptied the contents of his bag onto the plastic. The plastic did nothing to disguise the tone of each thump, which rang out in unique flutters depending on the size and shape of the object.

Human debris did not impress the rocks. The detritus left behind by humans lacked the rocks' own layered histories. The refuse that landed among them when the canal's currents lapped against their facets were mute and had no depth to their silence. The rocks did not know that the objects that pinged when they fell were house keys; the objects that echoed upon contact were jointed; and the objects that shattered were glass. They only knew from the heft of the objects that a myriad of weights pressed against them through thinly stretched plastic each time the Bone Man returned.

After the thudding of things, the rocks knew the Bone Man would lift the round object he always left resting among them. This round thing was an anomaly to the rocks. It was layered, yes, but it was nothing like them. With thin walls and a hollow inside, it was not made of a solid mass and its heft barely made an impression. Sometimes the man would ease the object over his head and sit in silence, peering—through two small holes— at his destroyed world. Sometimes he would hold the object in his lap and slap rhythms against its surface as the waters of the canal splashed noisily against the rocks at the bottom of the levee. Sometimes he screamed into the object, his voice bouncing around the inside of its globed interior before rushing back at him to slam against his face.

The rocks awaited the moment that the man quieted. He would turn the round object upside down and, balancing it on his knees, line it with plastic. Then slowly and methodically, he would press ripped strips of soggy paper against the round shape, mixing in small shards of debris to create a rough replica of the round hollow object. After carefully pushing the jumble of soggy items into a flat layer, he put the object aside, leaving it out to dry as he did what the rocks did not like him to do: draped himself across their facets, smothering the breeze and falling into a deep, dead sleep.

After the Bone Man discovered the sleeping child, he had a new obsession. He rose every morning thinking of the children. He stopped his daily attempts to cross the bridge and instead tried to rescue the children. His life conformed to a new rhythm, still perforated by heartbreak, still hounded by failure. There was no relief from the grief of rousing a new child from slumber and quickly losing the child to a ravenous patch of water.

One morning, he did not rush down the levee to search for another child. He was unsure of himself. His certainty of escape—for himself and for the children—was destroyed. He stared at the paper maché masks he had made. If nothing changed, he thought, his masks would cover the levee, stretching out as numerous and empty as the destroyed plots of land.

On impulse, he grabbed a mask and tucked it in the crook of his arm before running down the grassy slope of the levee. The globe shape of the mask forced his elbow to jut out at an awkward angle, causing him to he totter as he picked his way through the debris in search of a plot he had not yet visited. He navigated the wreckage, fingering the mask's uneven surface—the rub of his skin against the water-stained photographs, mud splattered letters, nails, and ground glass embedded in the mask distracting him from his impending failure.

When he finally selected a plot to plow through, he traced the sign of the cross over his body as he picked his way to the concrete stairs. Despite his fear of failure, he did not hesitate to launch himself up the stairs and bound onto the platform with as much force as he could muster.

He did not allow himself to get distracted by the coolness that bathed his skin as he plunged into the invisible walls surrounding the platform. Moving as quickly as he could, he squatted above the sleeping child, but when he grasped her shoulders to lift her, his hands went straight through her. He dropped the mask and snatched his hands away from her body. He recoiled in momentary shock. Then, just as quickly, fear of losing her seized him. He bent to scoop up the mask at the same instant the child started to stir. Her eyelids fluttered and she pushed herself up to sitting. Hands shaking, he glanced up at the sky. Before the child could collect her grief, the Bone Man slid the globed mask over her head.

For a few seconds, there was silence. The mask swiveled right, then left as she took in the disaster surrounding her. The Bone Man tensed as she gulped a huge breath of air and let out a wild yell. He pitched his head back, frantically searching the sky, but it was empty. He looked back down at the girl to see that she was rocking back and forth, grabbing at her chest as if it were being ripped open.

"You will not survive like this," the man yelled, his eyes flicking upward nervously.

"It hurts," the child said, her voice muffled and moist in the confines of the mask.

"You can't let it in. Bundle it up, wrap it tight so the hurt can't touch you."

As the girl continued wailing, the Bone Man was relieved to see that the mask muffled her grief, softening the volume of her cries. Along with her hushed wailing, a mist began to emanate from the girl. The man scooted backward, watching the mist seep from beneath the bowl of the mask and crawl over the child's skin. He was wary as the mist covered the platform until he could no longer see her. A large shadow passed overhead, but the patch of water did not stop and hover. In its wake, a gusty breeze swept across the platform, thinning the mist. Even so, the girl's howls grew more ragged and her panic more palpable. She began to convulse.

"I need my seizure medication," she yelled in a deep voice that was not her own.

"You ain't sick," the man yelled back.

"The attic is filling fast. The water's gon get me," she whispered in another voice.

"That attic's gone, girl. Ain't no more water neither."

"I can't get no higher. I'm already on the roof. Ain't nowhere else to go."

"You on the ground, girl."

But the girl did not heed him. She flailed around as the grief consumed her. The man searched the sky again, then reached out to comfort her, but there was only air where there should have been flesh. He pressed his palms flat against her back as if she were one of the ghost houses made of light.

"Breathe," he told her. "You ain't survive the storm to let what's left drown you."

She softened and calmed under his touch. Finally quiet, she rocked back and forth as if a silent terror was tearing her apart.

"All that you feeling, you got to carry it. Lift it up and let it ride your shoulders."

She went quiet, then she clenched her fists and started straining, heaving at the grief.

"That's right," he said. "Push it away. It ain't healthy to let it get in too deep."

After a few seconds of struggle, her shoulders collapsed. The Bone Man wet his lips to speak, but before he could offer an encouraging word, she took a few noisy gulps of air, straightened her back, and tried again. Her shoulders collapsed a few more times, but the man stayed silent as she pushed against the pain.

Before the Bone Man's eyes, the girl began to gain control. The formless mist that had surrounded her began to twist around itself, forming into wispy tendrils. The voices that had been bursting from her compressed into the tendrils and they began to whip around, circling her body in dizzying revolutions, screeching their desperation, hunger, and rage.

Finally the girl was completely still. The man scooted closer, staring at the voices as they overlapped each other, enclosing the girl in a blurry cloak of constant movement. He squinted at the mask, as if by staring into the eye holes, he could see her face.

"Who are you?" the girl whispered. The softness of her voice cut through the panicked voices that cycloned around her.

The man grabbed his chest as if shocked. He spread his arms, a wide grin creeping across his bony face.

"How you don't know me?!? I'm the Bone Man."

The girl eyed him, her expression obscured by the globed mask the Bone Man had used to cap her grief.

"You ain't from the 9th Ward."

The Bone Man laughed. "My daddy used to live here. I'm famous in Treme."

The girl looked around. The Bone Man could see the mask swivel from left to right as she examined the debris around them.

"They got people left in Treme?"

Before the Bone Man could answer, the girl convulsed. The voices around her abruptly halted their swirling and sank into her skin. A piercing shriek seeped from beneath the mask. She clenched her hands, took a few breaths, and straightened her back. He watched her force the grieving voices to slip out of her skin and resume their swirling. The Bone Man nodded his approval.

"You strong, girl. What they call you?"

"Trina."

"This your house?"

The globe swiveled left and right again.

"Used to be."

The Bone Man nodded as if with those three words, Trina had told him everything he needed to know about her. He stood and stretched out his legs.

"Let's go," he said with his hands on his hips.

The globe tilted backward as she looked up at him. The absence of buildings and trees made the sky his only background. Forgetting that she was not made of flesh, he reached his hand out to her.

"Come with me."

She did not move. He let his hand fall; it slapped against his thigh.

"You got something better to do?" he asked.

Trina did not speak. He could see that she was battling the voices again. When she had pushed them away and made them swirl again, she tugged at the blur of voices as if it was fabric. Pulling the cyclone of voices over her knees, she struggled to her feet. The Bone Man paused as she looked around, swaying unsteadily. When Trina had gained her footing, he led the way down the stairs. She kept a tight hold on the voices as she descended the stairs behind him, careful not to trip over them as she walked.

The Bone Man kicked at the debris that surrounded the stairs to clear a wider path for her.

"You staying close?" he asked as Trina followed him away from the remains of her family's home. He looked back at her repeatedly, keeping a close watch as they passed the ransacked remains of her neighbors' houses.

After they had put a few blocks of wreckage behind them, Trina said, "You ain't famous."

The Bone Man smiled, his gaunt cheeks lifting.

"I am and I'm gonna prove it to you," he said and slowed to walk next to her.

"Maybe you was famous. But ain't nobody left to be famous for."

"You think the whole city dead?"

"You see anybody else out here?"

The Bone Man stopped at the base of the levee. He reached for the globe covering her head.

"Only for a second," he said, and lifted the mask off her head. Trina blinked, adjusting her eyes to the daylight, then she gasped. The shattered houses and mounds of rubble were still there, but now the streets were clogged with people. Cars crept down the streets, gliding past the destruction; people waded into the debris, cameras dangling from their hands; a block away, Trina could see tour buses unloading more visitors.

"The city didn't die?" Trina's voice was hollow with disbelief.

"*They* city ain't die," the Bone Man said and started climbing the levee, but Trina didn't move. He pointed to the top with his chin. "We going up."

Trina stared out into the debris, her eyes—hazel and widely-set in a sandy-colored face—were unblinking. As she took in all the activity, the swirling voices stilled, slipping under her skin for an instant before she regained control.

"What they doing here?" she finally asked.

The Bone Man looked out at the people. After the streets had been cleared, when he'd seen the first cars crossing the bridge and driving into the neighborhood, he'd thought they'd come to rebuild. He expected cranes and shovels, dump trucks and building plans, but no one had come to clean or clear, they had come to record and gawk.

"Let's not talk about them today," he said after a loud, long sigh.

"But ain't nobody come to the 9th Ward before," Trina said.

The Bone Man could hear the indignation in her voice. The voices seeped into her skin and her chest began to heave.

"They gon leave us here," she shrieked in a high-pitched voice.

The Bone Man raced to her side and slipped the mask back over her head. Her whole body began to shake as if to throw off the mask.

"Shhh," he said softly. He placed his hands flat on her back and hoped she could feel his warmth. "It's done, honey, it's done. We can't change it, so don't let it take you over."

Trina suddenly turned away from the wreckage and pushed the wailing out of her body. When she got a firm grip on the voices, she looked up the levee.

"Why are we here?"

"Getting ready," the Bone Man said and began to trudge up

the levee's slope. Trina followed, fidgeting with the drape of voices around her ankles as she ascended.

"Ready for what?" she asked.

From the top of the levee, the Bone Man pointed down at the masks balanced in the nooks between rocks.

"Getting ready to keep the city going."

"You said the city ain't die."

"I said *they* city ain't die. If I can't do my job, *our* city might never get back on its feet.

The Bone Man pointed again and gazed proudly at his collection of masks.

"You made these?" Trina's hands lifted up to the globe encircling her head.

"Yep." There seemed to be a hundred of them nestled in the rocks below.

Trina paused.

"How long I been asleep?"

The Bone Man took a few steps down the wet side of the levee and rested his weight on the rocks.

"You don't know what today is?" he asked, looking at Trina over his shoulder.

Trina shook her head, the mask rotating back and forth.

"You can't smell it in the air?"

"Smell like death."

"It's Lundi Gras."

"You mean it's been..." she fell quiet for a few seconds. "... six months?!?"

The Bone Man nodded his head silently.

"This mess been here for six months?" Trina waved her hands around as she spoke. "And I... I been where you found me for..."

The Bone Man carefully twisted around to face Trina.

"Don't drive yourself crazy thinking about that," he said his arms outstretched as if trying to reach her from a great distance. "I need your help."

"My help?"

"I need you to help me get the other kids," he said, climbing across the rocks to the collection of masks.

"What other kids?"

"You think you the only kid that got left behind?" he asked, picking up one of the masks and passing it to Trina. A musty odor wafted from the mask and she held it away from her face.

"Ewwwww, is this what I'm wearing?" She peeked inside the mask. There were water-warped photos and handwritten letters plastered inside. She flipped it over and saw black rimming the eye holes and crude teeth drawn where a mouth would be.

"Ewwww, nothing! I made them with my own two hands."

"What for?"

"I'm the Bone Man," he said.

"How many times you gon say that?" Trina asked.

"Until you remember," he said. "Now let's go back."

"Back where?"

"Up," the Bone Man said firmly, pointing to the top of the levee.

Trina started climbing. The Bone Man grabbed a mask and followed close behind. Near the top of the levee, Trina wobbled. The Bone Man instinctively reached out to support her, but his hand went straight through her shoulder. She froze.

"You a ghost?" she asked.

The Bone Man shook his head slowly. In the silence, Trina dropped the mask and looked at her hands.

"Me? I'm a ghost?"

The Bone Man shrugged. "Can't say. Don't make no difference to me. The storm ain't leave none of us the same."

Trina lurched forward, holding her hands in front of her face. The Bone Man reached to comfort her, then stopped short.

"Whatever you are, there's more like you. Down there," he said, pointing at the wreckage. "Let's go free them."

"Free them for what?" Trina asked. "They sleep. They ain't got no idea what's happening out here."

"What if something happens to them? Sooner or later they gonna have to come and clear out these splintered up houses. What'll happen to them then?"

It was Trina's turn to shrug.

"Help me," said the Bone Man. "Help me free them and I promise I'll help you figure out what you are."

Trina looked out at the rubble, squinting as if staring at it directly would rip her apart. She picked up the mask and bounced it in her palms. The Bone Man watched her for any sign of agreement, but she only sighed. When she started walking down the levee, the Bone Man followed, not daring to speak another word as he descended in her wake, moving slowly toward the wreckage below.

The rocks felt agitated. They had slightly shifted their balance to adjust to those thin, hollow globes the man had rested upon them. Now the globes were gone, their weight disappeared, and the rocks' collective heft had changed again. The imbalance was not drastic. The new balance was not off-kilter enough to signal that it was time to slip or tighten or tumble, but just slight enough to change the way the wind played over their contours, to change the sound the air made when it splashed against their facets and dove into the gaps between them.

Just before the night had begun to release its opacity, the Bone Man woke. He rose from the rocks, exhausted and excited. He changed his clothes, scaled the rocks, and paused at the top of the levee. Scattered across the grass were the children he and Trina had rescued. Lying limp and lifeless, their limbs were flung outward at odd angles, their heads obscured by his crude globe-shaped masks.

Under the Bone Man's watch, one of the children stirred. When the child stood, he saw his mask dangling from the child's hand. He rushed down the grassy side of the levee, leaping over the sleeping children as he sped faster and faster toward the child.

"Put it on," he whispered as loud as he dared. The child stared at him with a crooked smirk.

"Trina?" the Bone Man said, drawing close.

She nodded

"Put your mask back on," he said, glancing fearfully into the dark sky.

"It's not coming." Her smirk deepened as if she were mocking him. She pointed at him with her chin.

"Why you wearing that?"

The Bone Man looked down at his body. His torso and arms were covered in a black turtleneck, his legs were obscured by a dingy fur-lined apron. Across the bottom half of the apron, he had stitched crude renderings of skulls and the words "You Next." He touched the brim of his top hat.

"I told you. I'm the Bone Man." He glanced up at the sky again. "How you know it's not coming?"

"It came last night, but I just did like you said."

The Bone Man furrowed his brow. He did not know what to say.

"I didn't know I could call it and push it away," Trina said after a pause. Something cold and grim flashed in her eyes.

The Bone Man remained silent. He felt a terrible itch crawling over him—the itch insisted that nothing was right and nothing would be right. That this thing that had happened—the breaking of the levees—was the final blow that would sweep them all away: the unwanted, the stubborn survivors, the rabble rousers, the good-time makers, the keepers of the flame.

"Wake the children!" he yelled suddenly, as if through sound he could dispel the weight of defeat.

A look of confusion flitted across Trina's face.

"In the dark?"

The Bone Man pointed into the sky. Just beyond his finger, Trina could see the Claiborne Bridge looming large, it's rusty steel frame nothing more than a dark silhouette in the quickening dawn.

"We're crossing that bridge, we're going to Treme, and we're going to save Mardi Gras."

Trina laughed. The sound was short and sharp. "Save Mardi Gras?!"

"I got a job to do. Every Mardi Gras morning I wake the city, and if I don't..."

"If you don't wake the city? You gonna wake the whole city?"

The Bone Man shook his head. "I'm gonna go to Treme and do what the Bone Man do," he said testily.

Trina crossed her arms.

"You said you were gonna help me figure out what I am."

He stared at Trina, fighting not to look as shaky as he felt.

"I'm gonna help you."

"When?"

"Look, I don't have no magic powers. Only magic I know is in the masquerade."

"Well your masks stink!"

"They saved you, didn't they?"

Trina jabbed her finger at his chest. "If you ain't gonna help, you shoulda just left us where you found us."

"Nobody said I wouldn't help..."

"If you don't help, I'll bring the water." Trina yelled.

The Bone Man shook his head.

"It ain't smart to play with things you don't understand, lil girl."

Trina clenched her fists.

"I ain't playing. You dare me?"

"What I look like daring a child? You ain't never gonna find me daring a child to do something that's gonna hurt them."

"It ain't gonna hurt me, it's gonna get you."

The Bone Man took a step closer to Trina. His voice softened.

"The water don't want me. It wants you."

"You a lie!" Trina threw the mask on the ground.

"What I got to lie for? It come down, suck kids up, and fly away."

Before the Bone Man could say another word, Trina fell to her knees and began to bawl. Her cries shot up into the sky, echoing in the darkness. The Bone Man scooped up her discarded mask and eased it over her head. Then he stood over her and watched her rolling around in the grass, rocking her head back and forth as she cried.

"Can't win for losing," he muttered to himself. "Maybe I ain't supposed to save these children. For all I know, this they place and the water just doing its job, keeping them where they belong."

"I don't belong to no greedy patch of water," Trina yelled. In that instant, the calm dark of the sky was ripped apart by lightning, bright flashes of light accompanying each of Trina's words.

The Bone Man flinched, crouching low while working to look less terrified than he was. "You don't know where you belong," he said, forcing his voice to ring out authoritatively. "Don't nobody know nothing no more."

Trina sat up suddenly.

"Don't leave me here," she shrieked.

"Then stop acting a fool."

Trina quieted her cries and started to sniffle.

"You done?" the Bone Man asked.

Trina nodded.

"Good. Go wake the children."

He reached down to help her stand, then withdrew his hand before she could see the gesture. He paced as Trina walked among the children to wake them. When awake, they stood in scattered rows, swaying and unsteady on their feet. Their masks—haunting and familiar—glowed faintly in the early morning dark.

"It's our day," he said to himself. Then he yelled it aloud, his wrist snapping as if he were flicking a tambourine. "It's our day."

Each little head turned in his direction and they stared at him through black-rimmed eye sockets. He flung his arms outward and pointed to the children. "Today you are Bone Men. We gon wake the city and we gonna let them know we're still here."

For a split second, everything receded—the debris disappeared and he pretended he could hear his Bone Crew roaring back at him—banging on their cowbells, amen-ing his words, raising their bones in the air in anticipation of the journey to come. A splinter of peace pushed through his anguish, and he gave himself to the ritual: the anticipation of creeping through dawn, his skull-masked gang raising holy hell behind him as the last vestiges of moonlight glowed on their masks. The children leaned together, whispering to each other, reminding the Bone Man that they were not his flesh-and-blood gang.

Anguish rushed back in. Doubt nagged at him, raging hysterically with dire warnings. *What if you don't make it? What if the bridge rejects you? What if you're leading the children to their deaths?* His breath caught in his throat then he shook off the questions.

"Ain't no way to know," he whispered to himself. He had no way of knowing if he was helping or harming; if the children trailing behind him were trusting or skeptical. "Ain't no way to know" became his new chant. He repeated it as he strode through the debris to beat back his desperation and disillusionment.

When he stood at the foot of the bridge, Trina at his elbow and the army of children at his back, he was momentarily frozen. The sound of the voices rustling around the children like so many tiny whirling tornados was maddening. He worked to push the sound away as he faced the fact that any choice he made in a world this destroyed could be sane or insane depending on the slipperiness of the moment.

"Are we sneaking?" Trina finally whispered.

He looked down at her.

"We'll see," he said, adjusting his top hat and stepping onto the bridge's concrete ramp. Trina matched his strides, keeping pace with a quick double-step that kept her close by his side. His repetition of "Ain't no way to know" returned as he made halting progress up the on-ramp. Sometimes the chant came out as a plea, other times as an indignant defense, but each time, it was a bid to hold on to his faith, to convince himself that the only way was forward.

His faltering progress confused the children. Each time he halted or hesitated, the children collided with each other and struggled to keep their footing. It was as if there were an undertow, dragging them all forward, then shoving them away.

At the top of the bridge, the air thickened, as if its molecules were swollen and threatening to burst. The Bone Man stepped onto the metal grate and the curtain of lights sparked to life. Gripped with an icy numbness, the Bone Man removed his hat and wiped his forehead. The children—a pint-sized swarm in skull masks that bobbed in the darkness—came to an abrupt halt behind him.

"What is that?" Trina asked.

"Something that wants to stop us," the Bone Man said.

"We gonna let it?" Trina asked. The curtain had begun to spark.

The Bone Man shook his head. "We can't stop."

Without another word, he crossed his arms over his face and threw himself at the curtain of lights. He expected to be flung backward, ruthlessly shamed in front of the children, but instead the lights sucked him in. The metal grate underfoot disappeared and the air around him filled with layers of gray mist.

He heard Trina yell, but he could not find her no matter which way he turned. Each time he tried to take a step, his feet slipped. He found himself stumbling through an unsteady nothingness, as if he were trying to walk on shifting waters.

"Bone Man!" Trina yelled.

He craned his neck backward toward her voice. That small movement flipped him backward. Suddenly, he was plummeting. He flailed his arms, grabbing at the air.

"Now," he heard Trina shout.

On that cue, a wailing rose up around him. He felt the children's cries wash over him, lapping at the air and growing stronger as their voices built into thick layers. He was still tumbling through the gray mist when the bridge began to rattle ferociously. Water droplets hurled past him, cutting ribbons of air through the mist. Each drop that whistled cleared a streak of space that he could peer through.

The children's assault turned the thick clouds of mist into weak tatters. Suddenly, he could see around himself. The children—focused and unwavering—were advancing across the bridge, swaying unsteadily as they propelled powerful cries into the air around them. Tears, leaking from the necks of the masks, dripped down the children's shoulders and plopped into the swirling voices that cocooned each of them. The voices splashed the water outward, pelting the Bone Man with droplets of unexpected force. Each teardrop that slammed into him knocked him backward and sent him spiraling through the mist. He curled into himself, folding his head toward his knees, crouching to hide from the barrage of droplets raining down around him. Peeking out from the shelter of his arms, he saw Trina part the curtain of light as if it were a flimsy nuisance, then his body slammed down onto the ground.

With the bridge suddenly solid beneath his hands and feet, he scrambled ahead, pushing past the children without knowing if they were advancing or retreating. He pressed his hands over his head as the children's tears continued pummeling. Finally he felt the bridge sloping downward beneath his feet.

"We made it," he heard Trina shout, but the pelting did not stop.

"Make them stop," he yelled, but his voice was obliterated by the wailing and sobbing.

"That's enough, ain't it?" he yelled again and stumbled blindly away from the spray of tears. He ran until he felt no more blows at his back, then he stopped, chest heaving and gasping for breath. Bruised and soaking wet, he turned to look at the chaos behind him. A proud smile spread across his face as he watched Trina slowly threading her way through the sea of children, stopping to whisper to each child. His gang—that ephemeral army of children—

had made it through to the other side. While Trina quieted them, the Bone Man allowed himself one solitary soft thought: Maybe the city that had a sham of an evacuation system, had built faulty levees, had closed ranks against him and his kind had a place for them after all. Maybe if they pushed hard enough, they could all—all the lost and dispossessed—get back to the other side.

He allowed the thought to fill him with warmth, then he looked around at the destroyed and decrepit homes around him. The cold reality filtered back in. No one had come for them in all this time—this ragtag band of children and these crude masks were all he had left of the city—and all the city intended to offer him. Trina and the sea of globe-headed children flowed toward him. He drew himself tall and strode off the bridge. His bedraggled, ghostly gang underscored the one thing he knew to be true: survival was his only birthright. Everything else seemed calibrated to conspire against him and his kind, and they were going to have to fight like hell to keep this city as their home.

The Second Surge

Beneath the battered boughs of trees, the children trooped behind the Bone Man down Poland Street. The trees stood silent. They were not surprised to find themselves standing upright, still lining the street in stately rows. Survival was in their lineage. They had the ancestral know-how to withstand whipping winds, surging floodwaters, and battering rain. Through their roots, they could foretell changes of weather. The coming of storms, the absence of rains, seasons of frost, none of it caught them unaware. Whenever the changes came, they tightened their roots, clung to the dirt, and suffered the loss of leaves, the breaking of branches stoically.

The trees drew strength from their history, and each time they had to withstand the destruction of their fullness, they suffered. For generations they had been tall solid presences. In the midst of shifting surroundings—from wilderness and marsh, to farmland, to concrete, and structures of wood—strength and solidity, the ability to proudly bear the marks of time was like currency among them. To be robbed of their marks of maturity, to have their majestic heights and impressive widths diminished was a grave dishonor, for what was there to revel in if the signs of growth that mirrored the years they had endured were erased? How else would they remember the seasons that had passed them by?

Bedraggled and wounded, the trees had no interest in the meanderings of humans. Nature had been parading its oddities before them for an eternity, yet these little people—heads capped with globed skull masks and bodies surrounded by swirling winds—were different. Taking the children as a sign of unfavorable conditions, the trees tensed their roots. They did not sense any atmospheric disturbances through the pulsing of dirt. The absence of tornado, hurricane, or windstorm confirmed, the trees rustled what leaves they had left and turned their attention skyward.

The trees would have taken even less interest in the children had they known that the swirling cloaking their little bodies was not a force of nature, but the collective voices of human grief—the grief of surviving the storm, the grief of losing the city, the grief of slipping away when the levees broke and the water came rushing in. Oblivious to the awareness of trees, the children were fascinated with everything around them. The globed masks swiveled back and forth as the children ogled the empty houses, the sagging porches, the veil of abandonment that smothered everything around them. Trina scooted closer to the Bone Man, working hard to match his purposeful stride as he led them down the sidewalk.

"How come they still got houses over here?" she asked. Her voice was indignant, as if the Bone Man owed her an explanation.

"Water wasn't as bad here."

Trina paused to see if the Bone Man would say more, but he just kept walking.

"So it ain't the whole city,"

"Nope," the Bone Man said without missing a step. "Ain't even the whole 9th Ward. Just depend on how close you was to where the levees broke. We turning up here."

Trina fell silent as they turned off Poland onto St. Claude. She stepped away from the Bone Man to keep a watchful eye on the children as they traipsed along, bumping into each other as they navigated the corner. When she was sure none of them were left behind, she ran to catch up to the Bone Man.

"What's that nasty, dirty line on all the houses?"

"That's the water line—how high it got."

"And that?"

Trina pointed at spray painted circles violently scrawled across the face of every house. He looked at the X that separated each circle into quarters and drew in a sharp breath.

"That's how they counted us. The number on that side show how many they found alive, that next one show how many was alive. Ain't no count for them that disappeared."

The Bone Man paused, waiting for Trina to start convulsing, but she remained calm. The swirling voices didn't sink into her skin and take her over. She kept a hard, unreadable expression on her face. Confident Trina wouldn't slip into crisis, the Bone Man trudged on in silence. At first he was proud of her for learning to control the voices, but suddenly he was drenched in melancholy. When a child had to push away her feelings, build herself into a fortress against anger and loss, there was nothing to celebrate. It was no more than he had done, but how could he rejoice that a child had quickly learned that she had to make herself a little more dead to survive.

They walked past discarded house after discarded house in silence.

"You think it'll come for us here?" she suddenly asked after they'd put a block or two behind them.

"What?"

Trina pointed to the sky and the Bone Man saw it all over again—the floating patch of water that had menaced her, threatening to suck all the children up and fly away with them.

He shrugged.

"Wish I could say I knew, but I don't. After Treme, I'm gon take you to somebody who can help."

He tried to look confident, but he was gripped by a sudden nihilism. He had clung to this one day for so long. Fixating on Mardi Gras morning had brought him through isolation, depression, confusion, but now he needed more than survival. He needed answers: How could he help Trina? What were the children made of and where did they belong? When Carnival Tuesday melted into Ash Wednesday, what was he supposed to do with his tomorrows?

"Look," he said when Trina lapsed back into silence. "We gonna figure it all out, but first, we're gonna have some fun."

Gathering up a bit of energy, he veered off the sidewalk and jogged up to a pale pink house. The children stopped short and watched as he bounded up cracked concrete stairs and flung aside a splintered screen door. The Bone Man hesitated. The house seemed to sag and bow inward as if protecting itself from another encroachment.

He balled up his fist and banged on the door. Trina motioned for the children to stay put and rushed up the walk to the house.

"What are you doing?" she asked running up the stairs.

"I'm doing what the Bone Man do. Waking everybody up on Mardi Gras morning."

He cupped his mouth with his hands and yelled "Wake up! Wake up!"

Trina stared into the Bone Man's face as if trying to determine if he was insane.

"Ain't nobody in there," she said.

The Bone Man banged on the door again. "It's Mardi Gras morning," he yelled. "You been good? If you ain't, I'm coming for you!"

He paused but there was no reply.

"I told you, you ain't famous," Trina whispered.

"This ain't Treme," the Bone Man whispered back. He

slammed his hand on the door. Both Trina and the Bone Man jumped when the door swung open.

"Hello?" the Bone Man yelled leaning into the house. The rank scent of mold rushed out of and exploded in his nostrils. He turned away and grabbed the porch railing. His body contracted as he was seized by an uncontrollable cough. Trina stared into the dark recesses of the house, then turned to watch the Bone Man struggle to catch his breath.

When the coughing subsided, the Bone Man drew in a huge gulp of air, pressed his nose and mouth into the crook of his elbow, and stepped into the house.

"You trying to kill yourself?" Trina asked as she stepped into the house behind him.

Slowly, as their eyes adjusted to the dark contours of the house, the silhouettes of objects made themselves known: water-stained couch, overturned lamps, a splintered coffee table. Trina noticed that even as the Bone Man swung his head around to check out the room, he kept his arm pressed against his nose and mouth.

"It stink in here or something?" she asked.

"Mold," the Bone Man said and pointed to the wall. There, stretching across the ceiling, spreading along the top of the walls, was black mold flourishing in large lacy clusters.

"If it stink that bad, the way you holding on to your face, can't nobody live in here."

Trina saw a plume of smoke rising from the corner.

"You see that?" she asked. She took a tentative step toward the smoke.

"What?" the Bone Man asked, gasping for air after he spoke.

"Who acting a fool now?"

The Bone Man hesitated. He took a hurried glance through the doorway that led to the rest of the house, squinting in the faint light that filtered into the house through dirty window panes.

Trina turned to face him. "You better get out of here before you be the next one dead."

With a sigh, the Bone Man turned on his heel and staggered out of the house. Trina turned back to the plume of smoke and crept toward the corner.

"You might as well go head and get on out of here too," a gravelly voice said.

Trina jumped. The voice cackled at the sight of her fright.

"He got you wearing one of his silly masks?"

A rush of loyalty overwhelmed Trina. She put her hands on her hips.

"This silly mask saved me. I rather wear a stupid mask than sit up in a broke down house hiding in the dark."

A clicking sound rang out, then a burst of light exploded from a lamp and streamed down on a large overstuffed chair. In the lamp's glare, a thin woman—gaunt and sharp-eyed—reclined on the chair. The wall behind the woman was splattered with grime, the chair's upholstery was overrun with mold, and the lampshade just beyond her shoulder was ripped and tattered.

Trina eyed the woman in silence, wondering how dead she could be with cheeks reddened with too much blush and a short blue dress that looked brand-spanking new.

"Well?" the woman said, when Trina didn't speak. She took a drag on a pristine cigarette she held pressed between her fingers and exhaled another plume of smoke.

"It's Mardi Gras day," Trina said. It was all she could think to say.

The woman burst out in laughter. When it tapered off, Trina could hear the bitterness of it burning her ears.

"Tell the Bone Man ain't nobody studying no Mardi Gras." The woman flicked cigarette ash to the floor and crossed her legs.

Trina couldn't help but stare at the large white satin bloomers that covered the woman's thighs all the way to the knees.

"What you starin at? Ain't you never seen a Baby Doll before?"

"Yeah, in my toy box," Trina said.

The woman rolled her eyes at Trina, took a noisy suck on her cigarette, and fell back into silence.

Trina crossed her arms. "Well what you want me to tell the Bone Man? You coming out?"

"A lil' raggedy parade in Treme can't do nothing for me. Ain't gon do nothing for you either."

"How you know?"

The woman lifted her arm and stiffened her fingers so that her hand made a flat surface. She slowly slid it across her throat. Her hand went straight through her neck as if she were made of air.

"I ain't dead," Trina yelled and turned on her heel.

The lamplight flickered and in a flash the woman had materialized in front of the door, blocking the exit.

"What? You think you special? Ain't nobody alive could sit up in this house as long as you been in here," she said.

Trina shook her head. "I ain't dead," she repeated. She said it slower this time so the woman would know she meant it.

"You try it then," the woman goaded.

Trina pulled the mask off and squeezed her fingers together. She pressed them to her neck, pushing as hard as she could against her skin, but her hand would not enter her flesh.

"I told you," Trina said and stuck out her tongue. "I ain't nothing like you."

The woman reached out as if to grab Trina, but Trina sprang forward, darting straight through her. Trina wrenched the door open and slipped out of the house, the woman's yells of "Carnival ain't gon save you!" ringing in her ears. She took the stairs at a sprint and kept running until she caught up with the Bone Man and the children. Before she returned to the Bone Man's side, she paused to tap the shoulders of the children, one by one. Their skin was cool beneath her fingertips, but like her they were solid.

"What? You counting them?" the Bone Man asked turning off to go down another walk.

"Just...checking them."

She watched him knock and yell at the house's closed front door before returning to the sidewalk.

"So?" the Bone Man asked, wading in among the children to push on to the next house.

"Oh, they all good," Trina said, stumbling forward to join him. The truth was, she didn't really know how they were doing. Under her touch, each of them had looked up at her, but their expressions were obscured by the blank features of the masks. They could be frightened or excited, angry or forlorn, but at least—she reassured herself—they weren't ghosts.

"I ain't talking about the children. The house," he said pausing to look at her. "You find something in that house back there?"

"A Baby Doll?" Trina said, her reply coming out more like a question than a statement.

"A baby doll? Now you collecting toys for the children?"

"No." Trina shook her head. "Not that kind. I saw a grown woman dressed up like a doll."

The Bone Man clapped his hands together. "Oh, you found a Baby Doll. Don't nobody cut up on Mardi Gras like the Baby Dolls. She ain't coming out?"

"She..." Trina paused. "She a ghost. But I'm not."

The Bone Man looked down at Trina, pity and sadness on his face.

"No, I'm not. See..." she said and pushed her hands against her neck. "I can't put my hands through my body—but that Baby Doll, she can."

"But I..." the Bone Man reached out to touch her shoulder, and once again, his hand went straight through her body.

"Maybe I'm part ghost," Trina said. "Just because I'm a ghost to you, don't mean I gotta be a ghost to myself."

For the first time since he'd rescued her, the Bone Man heard a hint of hope in her voice.

"Good. I'm glad you learning something about yourself," he said, then abruptly turned down the walk of a drab green shotgun house with peeling black shutters. "They got somebody in this one. I can feel it. You coming?"

Trina approached the house behind the Bone Man feeling like everything inside her was chaos. The discovery that someone was more ghostly than her thrilled her, but thrill wasn't all the Baby Doll left her with. The woman's bitterness hadn't infected her, not exactly, but the woman's skepticism amplified her own questions about the Bone Man's mission. Why did he think a Carnival parade would help? What was some tambourines and costumes going to do about the insistent loss pulsing through the city?

The Bone Man yelled "Wake up! Wake up! Mardi Gras Day!" loud enough to rouse anyone in the vicinity. Before he could knock, a teenager with neat cornrows and faded jeans opened the door.

"Ohhhhhhh," the teenager said when he saw the Bone Man and reached out to slap hands in greeting. Their syncopated handshake was a balm to Trina, a few seconds of normalcy in a world that had been destroyed beyond recognition. The teenager leaned his lanky length against the doorframe and gave the Bone Man a wide grin. "They let you back in the city?"

"I ain't never left," the Bone Man said, puffing himself up. "You been good?"

"Depend on who you asking," the teenager said and laughed. Trina caught a flash of gold in his mouth. He turned away and yelled, "The Bone Man here!" into the house, but the only reply was loud voices erupting in argument. The teenager rolled his eyes. "This all they do since the storm."

He leaned away from the door to yell, "Y'all ain't hear me?" then he walked through the living room and disappeared from sight.

The Bone Man stepped into the house. Trina entered behind him, taking cautious glances at the crease where the wall met the ceiling. The house had no mold; it was filled instead with Mardi Gras finery. Draped across the sofa were vibrantly colored panels of fabric. Lined up in neat rows on the floor were plastic bins holding multicolored jewels, sequins, and beads. In the corner, a staff—bejeweled and gleaming—rested against the wall.

From the open doorway on the other side of the living room came an explosion of sound. Trina followed the Bone Man toward the arguing voices. In the next room, two men were looking down at a map spread across a large antique table. Both men were costumed, but one was boldly plumed in bright blue. Feathers and beading, sequins and satin covered his entire body. Each detail of his costume was brilliantly colored and eye-catching. Trina stared, taking in his huge feathered headdress, velvet pants, and gloved hands before settling her gaze on the intricately beaded scene that adorned his chest. Covering his torso like armor, the beaded breastplate showed a red-skinned man walking across a wide blue swath of water.

Trina was staring at the swirling and churning of the water when the Bone Man let out a whoop.

"Big Chief! You made a new suit?!? Your crew suited up too?"

The men looked up from the table. For a few seconds, Trina feared they wouldn't speak. Their eyes were glassy as if they were disoriented by their arguing, by the Bone Man and Trina's sudden appearance, by the world around them.

In the quiet, the Big Chief squinted at the Bone Man. The two shiny black braids that framed his brown face were perfectly still.

"Bone Man," he said seriously. "We still here."

"Yeah, you right!" the Bone Man said, with the braggadocio inflection Trina had heard all her life. He reached across the table to slap hands with the Big Chief.

"We here," the second man echoed, "but it feels like we're the only ones to make it back."

The second man's voice struck Trina as grand and important. Looking away from the Big Chief, Trina found herself staring right at King Zulu. His white satin suit and the jeweled panel draped over his chest glimmered. Erupting royally from his shoulders was white decorative panel that fanned behind him, creating an opulent backdrop for his face. A short curly black wig covered his head and his skin was slathered in soot-black paint with the exception of a white circle painted over one eye and a white oval painted over his mouth. Every bit of his adornment was covered in gold embroidery, black jewels, and silver braiding that curled around and into itself in a majestic filigree. He too was feathered, but they were white, fountaining from his headdress, adding a foot to his height.

"That's King Zulu," Trina whispered.

The Bone Man nodded. There were a few seconds of silence, then without another word, both men looked back down at the table.

"It's about land," King Zulu said. He pointed a white-gloved finger at the map that was spread out on the table. His finger had landed on a red zone on the map. "Who do you think lives here and here?"

The Big Chief nodded his head, his headdress bobbing with each movement. "It's about the people on the land. Ain't no mistake who got wiped out."

"King Zulu," the Bone Man said, but King Zulu didn't look up. Instead he held up his hand as if to silence the Bone Man. When King Zulu held his hand across the table, Trina was suddenly engulfed in the smell of her grandmother's house. She could almost feel her grandmother's presence next to her and hear the blare of the television as they watched two kings of Carnival—Zulu and Rex—meet on Carnival Monday. King Zulu always outstretched a hand as he raised a toast to King Rex and the city as they ceremonially sparked the Carnival festivities. She had watched the ceremony with her grandmother for years, first passively, and then with bewilderment when the juxtaposition of King Zulu's mixture of blackface and refined pageantry, animal skins and jewels became clearer to her. Last year things had changed. The choreographed meeting of black and white masquerade didn't feel so innocuous.

Just a few months before, a spelling bee had taken her from the crumbling walls and chaotic hallways of her school into a school with gleaming hallways and a pristine auditorium. She had no words for the sensation that slowly washed over her when she understood the degradation she suffered at school daily was earmarked for her and her kind, but not for others in the city. The next time she saw King Zulu and King Rex she knew the masquerade was more complex and fixed than she'd imagined. Standing there in the cold Lundi Gras air, the two kings were not only playing at royalty, they were also playing at equality. The men—King Zulu in his short black wig and King Rex in his shoulder length curled blond wig—were equals in costume only. When they disrobed they would walk back into very different lives.

The Bone Man darted toward the table as another stretch of silence fell between the men.

"Money equals high ground," the Big Chief said before the Bone Man could speak. "That ain't nothing new."

At those words, Trina found herself spinning backward in time again. This time, she was much smaller and riding high on her grandfather's shoulders. Her grandfather was pointing at huge concrete cylinders that lined Claiborne Avenue.

"None of this was here when I was a kid. All that concrete ruined everything," he said waving his hand at the expressway overhead.

His words ran right past Trina as she shifted on his shoulders, looking around at people laughing loudly, smoke billowing from outdoor grills—everywhere a carnival of color and sound.

"We were making it back then," he said, sliding into a rant. "All our own shops, up and down Claiborne, until they built that thing straight down the middle." He'd pointed up at the expressway again and again, as if by pointing it out, he could shame it for the vitality and economy it had suffocated.

Trina had not heard another word because suddenly, in the middle of the swirl of activity, a Mardi Gras Indian staggered around, terrorizing the crowds. He was not beautiful and majestic like the Big Chief. He was erratic and disorderly, running in wide circles, his head thrown downward, threatening people with the horns that erupted from his feathered cap.

Now, in this quiet house in Treme, there was no Wild Man throwing himself around. No distraction from the beauty of the Big Chief and the story stitched on every panel of his suit. Intricately beaded, water-drenched scenes decorated his chest and shoulders, and hung from his waist.

"We have to balance the scales," King Zulu said emphatically, interrupting Trina's admiration of the Big Chief's suit.

"Y'all masquerading?" the Bone Man asked in the pause between King Zulu's assertion and the Big Chief's reply.

"Ain't you a simple fool," a raspy voice said from the door.

Trina looked up to see the Baby Doll leaning in the house's open doorway. There was another pristine cigarette pressed between her fingers.

King Zulu skewered the Bone Man with a stare and slammed his hand on the table. "Look at this," he said pointing down at the map.

"Can't talk no sense into him," the Baby Doll said. "He got a one track mind."

King Zulu reached across the table and grabbed the Bone Man by the arm, forcing him to lean in even closer.

"This my route," he said, stabbing his finger at the map. "What I look like parading through a ghost town?"

"Ain't nobody here to parade with you no ways," the Baby Doll said.

Trina felt a stabbing sensation rumbling in her chest. She lifted her hand and pressed her palm against her collarbone.

"We occupiers—that's what they think," the Big Chief said. "They glad we got wiped out."

"Yeah, we occupiers," the Bone Man said. "That means the only space we get is the space we take."

The stabbing sensation flared, whirling in Trina's chest before spreading flat and skittering through her body.

"Fuck 'em," the Baby Doll said and flicked ash onto the porch. "I be damned if I run around acting like everything's copacetic."

At that, Trina's chest jerked forward, then she collapsed into herself, stumbling backward as a ball of light shot from her body and exploded in the center of the room. Everyone lifted their heads slowly, then ducked down as the bright, blazing light broke into a shower of sparks. For a few seconds, the sizzling of the sparks swishing through the air was the only sound in the room. No one moved as the sparks rained down on them, burning holes in the map and leaving tiny marks on everyone's costumes.

Trina threw her hands over her face and skittered backward. She found a corner to press herself into as if by shrinking into herself she could disappear. King Zulu was the first to speak.

"She with you?"

The Bone Man nodded.

"Don't look like she belong here," the Baby Doll said before he could speak.

"I'm taking her to see Laveau," he snapped.

The Baby Doll shrugged.

"She might belong here, she might not," the Bone Man said, turning to the Big Chief and King Zulu, "but she ain't gon hurt nobody."

The Big Chief took a few steps toward Trina. "She look..." he paused and squinted at her. "...blurry or something."

"All of them like that," the Baby Doll said and exhaled smoke into the air.

"All of who?" King Zulu said.

The Baby Doll jerked her head in the direction of the front yard. Trina darted out of the room and rushed out of the house. The Baby Doll slipped out onto the porch behind Trina. King Zulu and the Big Chief slowly crossed the room to approach the doorway. They stood shoulder to shoulder in the doorway and silently looked out into the front yard.

The Big Chief let out a long low whistle. The children the Bone Man had saved were crowded around the porch, their masks knocking against each other as they fidgeted.

"What the hell is this?" King Zulu asked.

"Just some kids," the Bone Man said from behind them.

"Look more like an army," the Big Chief said.

"You taking them all to Laveau?" the Baby Doll asked.

"Yeah, and you need to go see her too," Trina said motioning to her neck.

"Gon be a lot for Laveau to handle," the Big Chief said. "I mean she good with spells, but you think she can handle this?"

The Bone Man shrugged. "Ain't nobody else can do it."

He squeezed past the Big Chief and King Zulu and ran down the stairs to join the children. "We going," he said and turned to work his way back to the sidewalk.

"Wait!" King Zulu yelled.

The Bone Man looked back to find King Zulu and Big Chief staring hard at each other as if a silent negotiation were taking place. Seeing these two men, men who had never walked alone, standing there marooned after being so violently severed from their people and left adrift in their own city retriggered the Bone Man's pain. He cut a less impressive figure than the two men standing in the doorway. He knew that as sure as he knew his name. He was an opener of the way, clearing space for the Big Chief's plumage and King Zulu's grand parade. Even in the best of times, his entourage had no flash. They had nothing more than a ragtag band of followers as they rambled about Treme until sunrise. Waking people and passing out warnings wasn't masquerading to some, but if he was going to trouble himself with what some people thought, he might as well have let the floodwaters take him.

"This could work," King Zulu muttered to the Big Chief, "but I need my..."

"Man, you ain't getting a float, not this year, and this the closest I'm gonna get to a tribe," Big Chief said.

King Zulu looked at the children's unsteady swaying skeptically.

"How we know they gon make the whole route?" he asked.

"How we know you gon make it without your float?" the Big Chief shot back.

"Ain't no route," the Bone Man said holding his hands out as if he were keeping the peace between them. "We just going in Treme to wake the people up."

King Zulu turned to the Big Chief.

"We here."

Big Chief nodded. "And what we here for if we ain't gon show the world how pretty we are," he replied, trilling his fingers across the face of his tambourine.

"I'm with you til my knees start complaining," King Zulu said as he slowly started walking down the stairs.

The Big Chief laughed, the beading on his breastplate glinting in the soft dawn light. "This ain't no luxury Mardi Gras, no. Ain't no pretty car gonna pick you up when you get tired."

"I got this," King Zulu said from the bottom stair.

The Big Chief banged out two sharp raps on his tambourine, then shook it so that it rattled. As the tambourine continued to vibrate, he leaned back and let out a war cry. Trina watched him descend the stairs, regal and stately in his blue plumage. When his beaded boot hit the sidewalk, he steadied the tambourine and started beating out a continuous rhythm.

Everyone faced him as he hunched over his tambourine and chanted, "Let's go get 'em." He rocked back and forth repeating the chant, nodding as the sound grew fuller and fuller as the Bone Man, King Zulu, and finally the children joined in. Trina slowly walked down the stairs toward the music. The Big Chief's eyes were closed as he started to sing the song lyrics between the chorus.

When the sound was solid, the Big Chief started to walk, drawing the children and neighbors down the sidewalk. She felt as if the music were tugging at her wrists and ankles, insisting that she join in, but she pushed the sensation away. Even as the sound slipped under her skin, she fought it. She was not a regular flesh and blood person. She was a problem and an impossibility. Trina pushed her way to the Bone Man's side.

"You think that lady gonna figure out what's wrong with us?" she asked pushing at her words so the Bone Man could hear her over the roaring sound.

He looked at down at her. They had traveled so far since the Bone Man had first woken her. He wanted to reach down and squeeze the haunted look out of her eyes and suffocate it with a big bear hug.

"Let's pretend," he said.

"Pretend?"

"Yeah, you know, like make believe."

"I quit make believe when I was seven." Trina crossed her arms.

He leaned closer to her. "Make believe is the only reason I'm here right now. I had to wake up every day and make believe I could make it across that bridge...even though, truth was—I couldn't. You got me across that bridge."

Trina leaned away from him as if suspicious.

"How come you couldn't cross that bridge? All those people in those big old buses crossed the bridge. Is you like us?"

The Bone Man shook his head. Her shifting and uncertain body must be a mystery to her, he thought.

He had no answers. He had only concluded that he was a little more alive than the children, but a little more dead than everybody else.

"So we ain't the only ones that need to go see this Laveau lady," Trina said into the Bone Man's silence

The Bone Man shrugged.

"About the make believe," he said. "Let's pretend this just a regular Mardi Gras."

Trina shot him a look.

"Worrying ain't gonna make the time fly faster." She walked along in silence, worrying at her lip with her tiny teeth.

He started an exaggerated clap in syncopation with the beat. "You know the song, let me hear you," he cajoled.

Trina didn't reply. He leaned closer and chanted *Let's go get 'em*, in her ear until a smile spread across her face. When she finally gave in and sang along, he winked at her. They sang together, exchanging looks and laughs for a few blocks. Watching the back of the Big Chief's suit bobbing up ahead, Trina asked, "You ain't mad?"

The Bone Man looked ahead to see King Zulu waving regally as he danced alongside the Big Chief.

"Mad?"

"Yeah. Ain't this supposed to be your thing?"

The Bone Man pointed at the people rushing out of their homes first in surprise, then in delight to see Mardi Gras royalty walking down the street.

"Do they look mad?" he asked. "Who's gonna be mad to see the Big Chief on Mardi Gras day? On *this* Mardi Gras day?" He waved his hand at the scene—the smiling faces in open windows and the skipping feet joining in with the procession. "This tell you everything you need to know. Mardi Gras ain't about me. It's about the people."

The Bone Man suddenly realized the size of their band of revelers had exploded. They were slowly parading closer to Esplanade, encountering more intact houses and drawing in more people to gather and amplify the sound. The energy ran through them, ping-ponging from body to body, transforming the people from abandoned and forgotten left-behinds into a many-handed, many-legged moving celebration.

When they reached Esplanade, the joyous shouts, foot stomps, dips, and handclaps had reached an ecstatic pitch. The Bone Man pushed his way to the front of the procession and pointed wildly.

"Turn here, turn here," he yelled. "We gon dip through Treme." Before he could redirect the revelers, a man stepped in front of the crowd, spread his feet wide, and blocked their path. The Big Chief stared at him, pounded out a few more raps on his tambourine, then let the song drop. The music fell to pieces, slipping away from the revelers and sparking a disgruntled fidgeting and grumbling.

"Flambeau," the Bone Man said, taking in the tall pole the man held hoisted over his shoulder and the flat metal board attached to the top. He was tall with the lower half of his face covered with a dark paisley patterned handkerchief and his legs clad in baggy dark denim. High over his head, three flaming torches protruded from the metal board, their fire blazing as bright as the ire burning in his eyes.

"What is this?" the Flambeau asked, his eyes wandering over the excited masses as he lowered the pole to rest it on the ground.

"Nothing you ain't seen before. You know how I do every Carnival."

"This ain't every Carnival that this year." The Flambeau adjusted a long string of dynamite hung around his neck.

"Every Carnival is the same to me," the Bone Man said. "The Bone Man got one job to do—one reason to be alive. The day I quit is the day I die."

"What are *you* doing out here?" King Zulu asked. "You're supposed to be lighting the way for night parades. What's a flame supposed to light while the sun is high in the sky?"

"Bone Man ain't the only one got a job to do," the Flambeau said.

King Zulu nodded like he understood, even though the Flambeau had not answered his question.

"Well, you trying to block the way, or you gonna let us get to it?" the Big Chief asked rattling his tambourine.

"My pockets light," the Flambeau said without shifting his stance.

"We all light this year," the Bone Man said spreading his arms wide. "You see my tribe anywhere? You see King Zulu's court? Ain't none of us got what we used to having. So why don't you just move to the side and let us pass?"

The Flambeau stalked in a wide circle, twirled his torch, and dipped down as if testing his knees.

"My pockets still light."

The Big Chief and King Zulu squared off as if preparing to challenge the Flambeau. Suddenly, there was the plink of a quarter hitting the ground at the Flambeau's feet. He did a quick step—feet flashing, knees flying—and scooped up the coin. Then more came, pinging on the concrete. When a few dollars landed nearby, the Bone Man helped him pick them up.

"You good now?" the Bone Man asked as the Flambeau was collecting the last few coins.

The Flambeau stood, hoisted up his pole, and said, "Let's go get 'em."

"Yeah, you right," King Zulu said.

The Big Chief slapped the tambourine. While the revelers were focused on syncopating their footwork to the beat, the Bone Man reached out and slapped hands with the Flambeau. Then, shoulder to shoulder, they turned and led the way into Treme.

"Hey nah!" a woman shouted as the agitation rose up again. The ragtag band turned down Barracks—the cheering and chanting carried everyone's feet far from the struggle of daily life.

Riding the energy, the Bone Man got a second wind. Winding his way through Treme's streets, he grew louder and wilder, throwing out his threats and warnings with relish.

Even as the band kept growing, the Bone Man stayed dedicated to his task, running up walks and banging on doors. Trina struggled to keep her eyes on him, and at the same time, to keep the children close. They bopped along with the band, the rambling energy of the procession sweeping them forward. Trina felt the Bone Man drifting further and further away, buoyed by the band. His teasing and cajoling of the revelers reached a fever pitch and Trina cut through it all.

"Bone Man!" she yelled.

The Bone Man looked down at her, disoriented. Snaking through Treme, the band had finally reached a fervor the Bone Man had worried he would never see again.

"They ain't get water here?" Trina yelled.

"What?"

"Water! They ain't get none here?" Trina repeated, pointing at all the intact houses.

"Just a little sprinkling from what they telling me," he said. "Why?"

"I don't see no black lines on the houses."

"I guess Treme was lucky," the Bone Man said.

Trina's face crumpled into a scowl. She had stopped believing in luck when she stopped playing make-believe. *What,* she wondered, *did Treme have that the Lower 9 didn't?* She remembered King Zulu's map—the patches of red and the parts that weren't touched by the floodwater. Must be some reason some folks got to live on high ground while other people's lives got buried under the weight of water.

She watched the Bone Man skirt a cluster of old ladies to dart down the walk of another house and turned back to the children. She kept the children safe and accounted for as the band ran through all the streets of Treme. At the iron gates of Armstrong Park, the Bone Man came to an abrupt halt. The crowd pressed at his back, wanting to surge onward.

Trina appeared by his side.

"What's wrong?" she asked.

He looked down at her.

"This is where I end."

"Is it like the bridge?"

"No," he smiled weakly. "My work is done."

Trina looked over her shoulder. There were revelers spinning, clapping, and dancing. "They ain't gonna let you stop now!"

The Bone Man hunched his shoulders and spread his hands as if he were powerless.

"Bone Man!" King Zulu yelled over the noise. "We done here. Let's take it to the water."

"King Zulu wanna bring it down. Trying to hang with the golden crown," the Big Chief slipped into his chant.

"Bone Man—I let you have this parade, now I say we take it up Canal," the Flambeau said. He shot the Bone Man a fierce and disgruntled look, and turned to weave through the crowd with fancy rhythmic footwork.

"Bone Man?" King Zulu said and pounded the Bone Man on his back.

Still the Bone Man did not speak, he just shook his head sadly. A block away, a coffee-colored woman in brown robes and a black nun's habit pushed the door to St. Augustine church open. She cocked her ears and was surprised to hear that she wasn't just imagining the sounds—there really was a celebration in the streets. She descended the stairs and, following the noise, she joined the crowd at the gates of Armstrong Park.

"Bone Man," she said after she had pushed her way to the front of the crowd.

"Sister DeLille!"

"Didn't think I would see you this year." She didn't smile as she greeted him. Her face was not angry, but curious. She slowly rotated away from him as she searched the faces of the revelers. "I sense some hungry souls."

"We're all hungry for something, Sister DeLille."

She snapped her gaze onto the Bone Man briefly, a slight smile alighting on her face.

"Yes, of course, that is why I serve our Lord," she said before returning to look out into the crowd. "This is different. It pulled me from my contemplation." This time her gaze fell on the masked children. "It must be the children. You carry on. I will care for them until you return."

The Bone Man shook his head.

"No, sister, I cannot leave them behind."

"They are hungry," Sister DeLille repeated.

The Bone Man glanced at the children. He was sure they did not eat, but this was not the time to dive into a conversation with Sister DeLille about the facts of their existence.

"They alright," he said. "I promise you." He looked around, worried about the crowd, but no one spared them a glance. They were writhing and jumping around, navigating the jumble of bodies with an unexpected deftness.

"I have a duty to soothe the souls of this city," Sister DeLille said drawing the Bone Man's attention back to her.

"Their souls? Didn't you say you wanted to feed them? I thought we were talking about food."

"Yes, I must feed them, but not with food. It is their souls that are hungry."

The Bone Man pointed in the air. "You hear that?" He bobbed his head to the beat of the Big Chief's chant. "That is what will feed their souls. That is the soul of our city."

Sister DeLille took a step closer to the Bone Man. She shook her head. "Our children are the soul of our city."

Watching Sister DeLille and the Bone Man's negotiations, Trina wondered what Sister DeLille could do. Could she really soothe them? Could she release them from this maddening limbo?

"If you will not leave them behind, then I will come with you," Sister DeLille said breaking the impasse.

The Flambeau, who was twirling his torch nearby, circled Sister DeLille. "Sister Delille, you gonna parade with us?!?"

"Of course, I will. I go where God goes and God is everywhere."

God, thought Trina. *What is God?*

It was a question she had asked repeatedly through the arc of her young life. God had not saved her from the violent horrors at school. God had not stopped her father from getting shot on the way home, bleeding to death. God had not stopped the city from flooding and her body from turning into...whatever she had become.

How, she wondered, *could God be everywhere.*

A sudden terror grabbed hold of Trina and she reached for the Bone Man's hand. When Sister DeLille discovered what they were, she was sure it would be confirmed that there was nothing Godly about her, especially not the ghostly bits.

Before she made contact with the Bone Man's hand, she remembered her condition, the impossibility of touch. Another wave of horror washed over her and she was forced to admit that no matter how close she felt to the Bone Man, she was another entity—something not human, something that had no precedent, and no reason for being—even in this water-soaked wasteland.

The Third Surge

Air molecules—nomads that they are—are not aligned on what sensations are most pleasing. There are those that prefer quiet and stillness, and others that love disruptions of any kind. When the city's heady celebrations of Carnival began to intensify, any air molecule that was inclined to avoid disturbances would slip away, leaving the city behind. The other—those that found the raucous days of Carnival to be intoxicating drifted into town specifically for the season's rambunctious eruptions of sound. There were so many opportunities to disrupt their equilibrium: the yells emanating from parade-going crowds, the laughter from party revelers, the scattered notes of music—forceful blasts from the tuba, rapid rat-a-tat trills from the drums, the sinewy snaking of electric sound tinkling from passing floats.

That there was less sound in the city this year was just common sense. The intense disruptions of that past August were temporary for the air molecules, but the residents didn't have the same ability to bounce back. With fewer noisemakers thrumming through the city, the visiting air molecules were on edge and their need for sound went unfulfilled. The Bone Man's crew bursting into Armstrong Park with an explosion of syncopation and agitation thrilled the gathered air molecules. They vibrated against each other as the sounds buffeted them about. The handclaps, foot taps, and joyful shouts created a compression and dispersion among them that made them gleeful with pleasure.

The outburst struck the ears of a trumpet player, a tuba player, and a drummer who had been milling about Congo Square. Before the procession even drew near, the musicians picked up their instruments so that the moment the Big Chief and King

Zulu strolled into Congo Square, they were primed to let out an impromptu blast of sound. The drummer began beating out a rhythm that spoke directly to the revelers' feet. Shouts went up as the tuba player joined in, throwing out deep growls that gave shape and body to the drummer's backbeat. The groove established, the trumpet player lifted his horn, pressed the mouthpiece to his lips, and blew a feverish riff that solidified the transformation. Just like that, the music slid from the Big Chief's Indian chants into a blistering second line.

By the time they flowed out of Armstrong Park, the revelers had become a river of sound. Cocooned by the music, they were momentarily freed from the interminable nightmare of trying to claw their way back home. As they rolled up Rampart, it was as if the city was theirs again. Their gathered bodies whipped into a frenzy of high stepping and hip swaying—they had become a blur of bodily incantations that refuted the existence of anything that wasn't kinetic and exultant.

At the next intersection, before the band could stall or splinter, Flambeau took the lead. He steered them down Canal, and they followed, confident in the power of their high-spirited, polyrhythms. They paraded past the grand, deteriorating buildings toward the river, but the alchemy of the music was as fragile as it was potent. At St. Peter's, a wall of people was their undoing. A crowd—facing the street with their hands raised, yelling wildly—blocked their path. The Flambeau stopped short and turned back, scrambling to find an alternate route, but it was too late. The mass of people and the discordant sounds up ahead punctured the band's ecstatic commotion. The Flambeau jerked his hand upward, as if with sheer strength, he could hold the strands of sound together, but they slipped through his fingers, disintegrating into half-strength notes, before falling apart completely.

When the second line died, reality rushed back in. The revelers were confronted with the sight of a huge float rolling down Canal Street. The parade-goers reached upward, hands raised, grasping for shiny doubloons, glittering beads, and plastic cups. The Bone Man's revelers were still in the shadow of the float as it rolled past them slowly like some lumbering beast. The men riding high, leaning over crowds to drop trinkets into people's palms extinguished their joy. The men's gleeful waves, their sequin-trimmed costumes were discordant notes in the sea of destruction the second-liners had been drifting through.

The float riders—with their blond wigs curled at the ends and their pink, slit-eyed masks—pained King Zulu more than most. Had it been any other year, his crewe would have rolled these streets first—leaving behind their own trinkets. Now King Rex's men were the first parade to greet Carnival Tuesday and the Crewe of Zulu was nothing more than a bit of history ground to nothingness beneath the wheels of the floats. King Zulu heard a dry chuckling next to him. He looked over to see the Baby Doll blowing smoke into the air.

"Look like the storm ain't slow the Rex crew down none," the Baby Doll said.

King Zulu did not reply. He crossed his arms and stood unmoving as beads from a second float flew through the air, arcing past the parade-goers and landing among the Bone Man's revelers. A yelp went up from the children and they darted around, scrambling to recover beads that had fallen to the ground. Whether they caught the beads in the air or rescued them from the ground, the children squealed with delight. Trina circulated among them while they chased beads down, offering a hand as they struggled to work the beads over the globed masks so the shiny plastic could dangle from their necks.

As a third float rolled into view, the Flambeau sprang into action. He elbowed his way through the crowd, clearing a space for the rest of the Bone Man's revelers to surge forward. The musicians followed and they all pressed against the police barricade that separated the crowd from the floats. The Flambeau leaned his pole on the ground and grabbed the prongs that connected one section of the barricades to the other. He jiggled the barricade until the prongs separated. He shoved a section of the barricade aside and stepped into the street. Before he could move into the stream of the parade route, Sister DeLille put a hand on his arm.

"We should not interrupt Rex's parade."

"I ain't studying Rex," the Flambeau said. "Our parade ain't over. These people need this second line. I need it."

The Bone Man squeezed between the revelers to work his way closer to the Flambeau. "Sister DeLille is right. This ain't our Mardi Gras. We don't even be over here on Carnival day."

"Speak for yourself, Bone Man," King Zulu said, "This is my parade route."

"And I parade anywhere," the Flambeau said. "Uptown, downtown, cross the river. Don't matter, I bring the flame."

"What y'all doing?" the Big Chief yelled from about a foot away. He was slowly coaxing people to stand back, so he could join the others without ruining the feathery expanse of his suit.

Watching him gingerly making his way through the crowd, Trina suddenly remembered the Wild Man. The way he charged the crowd to fiercely protect the Big Chief suddenly made sense. She skirted around him and started jostling the crowd to clear a space.

"What's all this conversation?" he asked when he finally reached their side. "If we don't get moving, we gon lose these people."

The debate rose up again. Trina leaned on the barricade next to the arguing adults, staring into the street as the children clustered around her. There was the sudden blare of bounce music blasting from the parade route. The driving beat slammed into Trina, jolting her to attention. She climbed up on the barricade and leaned over it to peek down street. From a few feet away she saw a banner that read: "9th Ward High Steppers" slowly coming near. Her excitement collapsed into confusion when she saw that the women proudly carrying the banner did not look anything like her neighbors. They wore hot pink short shorts and the shaking of their hips was more frenzied than fierce. Her cheeks grew hot as the realization washed over her. Everything about them—their furiously flailing white arms, their stolen choreography—was supposed to be a twisted version of her. Trina could see—in the women's ecstatic, smug grins—that they were thrilled to take the space black bodies usually occupied.

"This is not good for the children," Sister DeLille was saying as Trina raged silently.

"Why hide the truth," the Flambeau said. "This is what they do while the rest of the city has drowned."

"How can you judge when you are here masquerading too?"

"Sister," the Flambeau said, his entire body trembling with controlled anger. "This is no costume. I light the way to earn money to feed my family."

"I am sorry, my son, I only meant to say that it is hard to stop tradition."

The women continued whipping their way through their routine, oblivious of the effect their parody had on the ghostly brood that stood on the sidelines watching them. Trina's anger sparked, causing the back of her neck to burn. Her skin started to emit a soft crackling sound that silenced the children and activated the same crackling in their skin. The adults fell quiet and turned to look at the children. The Bone Man was the first to speak.

"I have to get them to Laveau—quickly."

Sister DeLille crossed herself.

"Not while God is my Father! You will not take them to see that witch!"

Before the Bone Man could explain himself, the children began to spark, tiny bursts of light shooting outward from their chests and ricocheting off their tightly packed bodies.

"Let's go *now*," yelled King Zulu. "Before the next float comes."

The Bone Man drew close to Trina.

"What's wrong with them? Can they walk?" Then he noticed Trina's face. Her brow was clenched, her nostrils were flared. "Trina? What's wrong, girl?"

The Bone Man waited for a reply, but Trina did not answer. Instead, she and the children started to tremble. The Flambeau ducked, wielding the flat board atop his pole like a shield as sparks flew off the children's bodies faster and faster.

"We need to move," he said and stepped into the street. The Bone Man crossed the barricade and followed the Flambeau into the street. King Zulu joined them, pushing the police barricade aside to clear a wide opening for the children. At the Bone Man's urging, Trina stepped into the street and the children stumbled after her, flooding past the barricades with a rush of musicians and revelers into the street. Sister DeLille stood back, watching the haphazard band swarm the street.

The Big Chief paused at her side. "You said you would walk with us, Sister."

She clasped her hands tightly under her chin "How do you know they aren't demons?" she whispered.

"They're children," the Big Chief said.

"But how do you know?"

"I know because you are here, Sister. Not even demons could call you from your contemplation, only the purest of souls. Do you sense evil in them?"

Sister DeLille unclasped her hands and held them out as if testing the air. She shook her head.

"They are children," the Big Chief repeated. "Our children," he said after a pause.

Sister DeLille smiled and squeezed the Big Chief's hand.

"You're a good man. You deserve your crown."

The Big Chief nodded in silent thanks, then motioned to the street.

"Are we going to let them leave us?"

Sister DeLille looked out into the parade route and saw the Bone Man stalking past the crowds as if they had gathered just for him.

"You living right?" he was yelling. "You better live right or you gonna come with me."

"You know, after all his masquerading, there's not been a Mardi Gras yet that he didn't come to me after he's done waking up Treme. I give him breakfast, and we talk. He tells me about the children he's guiding, what he's giving up for Lent..."

"You *know* he's gonna need somebody to talk to after today."

Sister DeLille sighed. The Big Chief stepped to the side, giving her space to join the others. When she finally entered the parade route, he followed close behind. By the time they caught up with the band, music filled the air once more. Canal Street had more space than the sidewalks and narrow throughways of Treme. Yet here in the open space, their celebration held more desperation than abandon.

The Bone Man's dire warnings grated against the musician's passionate attempts at revelry. He drew mixed reactions as he yelled out his predictions of doom. "All this is going to melt away," he shouted and some of the parade-goers whooped and clapped, trying to draw him near. "You better be ready cuz you next," he yelled and other parade-goers shrank away.

In the midst of his theatrics, the Bone Man heard a yelp. He whirled around to see that the light sparking from the children's bodies had grown stronger and more erratic. For a few seconds, the Bone Man was still as he watched the light shoot upward, arcing over the children to smack against the parade-goers' heads. The Bone Man's mouth opened in shock when he saw the parade-goers go stiff, their faces crumpling into sadness the moment the light showered down upon them.

He was drawn away from the spectacle of the sad parade-goers by the sudden realization that the children had gone quiet. He looked around to see if the others had noticed what was happening to the children, but everyone had fragmented and was drifting along in their own solitary worlds. King Zulu was strolling along the margins of the parade route, reveling in the attention of the crowds and waving grandly as he strutted by. The Big Chief walked with his head lowered. His scowl underscored his refusal to show off his feathered suit. Sister DeLille kept her fingers gripping each other tightly and her eyes down cast, praying as she walked. The Flambeau flung himself around, frantically high stepping and dipping low as if he could cajole the crowd into throwing tips with the complexity of his dance moves.

While the Bone Man was taking a closer look at the children, the Baby Doll materialized next to him.

"Something ain't right with them children," she said.

"They ain't doing nothing to you," he replied, bristling as if he and the Baby Doll were in the middle of an argument.

"No, I mean something's wrong with them. Look." The Baby Doll pointed to the children. The Bone Man saw that Sister DeLille was circulating between them, a worried expression on her face.

"Listen," the Baby Doll said.

The Bone Man cocked his ears and heard a soft gurgling coming from the children.

"Sound like they drowning," the Baby Doll said.

Trina grabbed the mask of the child closest to her and tugged it upward.

"No!" the Bone Man yelled. "You can't!"

Trina cut her eyes at the Bone Man and yanked the mask off the child. A stream of water tumbled from the mask. The child gasped, sputtering to grab a breath as the water streamed over his body. He leaned over, struggling to draw air into his lungs. He sucked in a big gulp of air and let a whispered "Thank you" slide out with his exhale.

"You can't do this," the Bone Man said, glancing fearfully into the sky.

"I *can't* watch them die!" Trina replied. She looked around wildly at each of the adults.

"Help!" she yelled as she rushed around, pulling masks from the children as quickly as she could.

The Bone Man watched, helpless to extinguish the terror that Trina would be the death of all of them. He felt his control of the moment slipping away as more and more children—freed from their masks—stood in place shaking and seeping water from their skin. Trina was frantically touching their shoulders, their faces, their necks, searching for the source, but she could not stop the water from flowing freely and dripping down the children's bodies to pool at their feet.

Once it hit concrete, the water spread, oozing across the street to collect under the crowd's feet. The touch of the water on their shoes transformed them. Spectators who had just been under the thrall of adrenaline, deliriously jumping in the air, squealing in delight as they fought for trinkets, were now hunched over in misery, moaning and pulling at their hair. The Baby Doll threw her hands over her ears as their wailing swelled. The Flambeau waded over to the Bone Man.

"They gonna drown everybody," he said, his voice caught between complaint and awe.

In the midst of all the commotion, King Zulu noticed the Big Chief prancing ahead with high agile steps.

"Big Chief, everything is going wild and you finally getting in the spirit?" he yelled.

"I'm not dancing for these fools," he yelled back. "I'm just trying to keep my suit dry."

King Zulu looked down. His shiny black shoes were covered in water.

"Float's coming!" the Baby Doll shouted.

"We need to get these children away from here," Sister DeLille said to the Bone Man.

The Big Chief was the first one to reach the barricade at Decatur. He grabbed it, jiggling it at the joints until the hooks came apart. The Flambeau was right behind him, twirling his flames wildly to chase away onlookers and clear a space for the others. Sister DeLille ushered the children forward while the Bone Man faced the crowds for his final warning.

"High ground won't save you," he proclaimed, lifting his hand as he backed out of the parade route. "You next," he said, pointing to parade-goers as he departed. "And you and you and you. You all next."

Upon leaving the parade route, the band transformed again. The high stepping they had started in Treme had devolved into a shuffle, and the musicians' spirited sound had dampened into a dirge. They trudged down Decatur, away from Rex's parade, feeling the friction of roving groups of Carnival celebrants circulating around them in their drift toward the French Quarter.

"Anybody else feet hurt?" the Flambeau asked when the musician's instruments finally fell silent.

"Not my feet. My ankles. They burning," King Zulu said.

"Mine on fire," the Big Chief said.

The Bone Man stopped and looked down at his feet. Water droplets covered his shoes and water had darkened his pants from hem to shin. He tugged at his pants leg and lifted the cuff, bending down to scratch at his skin. His eyes widened and he stood up in shook.

"Sister DeLille?" he said, calling her over.

When he lifted the hem of his pants, Sister DeLille saw red welts circling all the way around each of his ankles. "Look like the water gave you a nasty burn," she said, but then she looked closer. "What is that?"

The Bone Man crouched down. There, cutting right through the welts, was a dark line that zig-zagged up and down his ankle like a wave.

"What the hell?" the Flambeau said. He leaned his pole on a nearby building and lifted the hem of his pants. His ankles were marked—just like the Bone Man's—with red welts surrounding what seemed to be a tattoo of a wave inked on each ankle. There was a loud clatter as everyone—the musicians and the impromptu revelers—dropped instruments and flung off shoes to take a look. Oblivious to the strangers stumbling around them, they blocked the sidewalk, chattering hysterically. In the clamor, King Zulu found the same mark on his ankles. By the time Sister DeLille tugged at her stockings to find the rise and fall of floodwaters inked on her ankles, everyone was glaring at the children.

"Stop!" yelled the Bone Man, silencing their angry shouts.

"Is this ever coming off?" a woman demanded. The Bone Man felt a presence by his side and look down to see that Trina had sidled close.

"Did they do this?" a man asked, pointing to the children.

The Bone Man spread his hands futilely. "I don't know."

"If they dangerous, you can't be pulling people out they house to parade with them," the woman said.

The Bone Man looked her over. Her hair was tied in a handkerchief and she had buttoned a coat over her nightgown and thrown on a pair of jeans underneath. She'd probably come running out of her house when she'd heard them passing by.

"So you don't know nothing?" the man asked.

The Bone Man didn't know what the storm had put them through, how any of them had survived. He had come parading by with hope, now here they were with wet feet and tattooed ankles in a city that was becoming harder and harder to recognize as home.

"Well, don't matter if he got answers or not," the tuba player said. "I sure as hell ain't sitting around, waiting to find out what's coming next. Y'all out?" he said to the trumpet player and the drummer.

"Yeah, bruh. We with you."

The children gathered tightly together, cowering as the revelers left, reconfiguring themselves into small groups before disappearing back up to Canal, or down Decatur, or across Bienville and back into Treme.

When the crowd had left, only the Big Chief, King Zulu, the Flambeau, Sister DeLille, and the Baby Doll remained. The children stayed huddled around the Bone Man as if he could keep them safe.

"Y'all ain't scared?" the Bone Man asked.

The Flambeau shook his head. "Shit, you just saved me a trip to the tattoo shop."

"You got us out on Carnival Tuesday, man. This Mardi Gras would have been nothing but me yelling at this fool, if you didn't show up," King Zulu said.

"We gon stick with you til you get these kids to Laveau," the Big Chief said, grabbing the Bone Man by the shoulder.

Sister DeLille took a deep breath and covered herself with the sign of the cross. "I'm staying too. Somebody has to look out for you when this is all over."

The Big Chief rapped on his tambourine. "So we rolling?" he asked. When the Bone Man nodded, he let out a long, low moan that slid into a new chant.

"Shallow water, oh Mama," he sang and everyone fell in, lifting his chant.

They lacked the electric energy of the musicians and the restless surge of the revelers who had pushed the procession onward. The Flambeau took the lead again, urging them forward to the river. Their progress was slow as they navigated the clogged streets. Near Jackson Square, they had to push past all manner of silver robots and feathered dragons, shiny clowns and swamp creatures who staggered in and out of their procession in a relentless push toward the festivities.

Somewhere between Jax Brewery and Café du Monde, the Big Chief's steady call faded away. The Bone Man left the group in Café du Monde's courtyard, and doubled back. Retracing their steps, he was startled to discover that the Big Chief did not disappear alone. The Flambeau and King Zulu were also nowhere to be found. When he returned to the courtyard, Sister DeLille grabbed his arm.

"Forget about Laveau," she whispered. "Bring the children back to the church and stop making a spectacle of them. I will bless them and with God's grace, we will drive out whatever demons are controlling them."

"Sister DeLille, I..."

Trina interrupted their conversation, slipping between them.

"What happened to the rest of the city?"

Both Sister DeLille and the Bone Man looked down at her. The question was too big for a quick reply.

"What happened to what?" the Bone Man asked.

"The rest of the city!" Trina said louder. A sharp crackling sound accompanied her words.

"What do you mean 'what happened?'"

"I thought the city was destroyed. I thought there was no one left." Her words held a chilling calm that hinted at restrained rage.

"What? You talking about all these people?" the Bone Man said, motioning to the costumed hordes roaming the streets. "Most of them don't live here. And them that do, had to leave too. Lots of people came back."

Trina shook her head. The rest of her body was perfectly still as if she was rooted in place.

"These buildings never fell. The rest of the city survived?"

"It was bad all over," Sister DeLille said, "And people are still hurting all over the city."

The Baby Doll circled the three of them and stopped next to Trina.

"Don't let them sell you that, girl," she whispered in Trina's ear. "Everybody ain't suffer the same."

Trina begin sucking in big gusts of air and shooting them out of her mouth. Her chest displayed her agitation, rising and falling dramatically with each inhale and exhale. The Bone Man shot an angry glare at the Baby Doll.

"Stop egging her on. You keep messing around and we all might get washed away."

"Can't drown twice," the Baby Doll said shrugging.

The Bone Man kneeled so that he was eye-to-eye with Trina.

"Trina, you need to breathe," he said.

"You ought to let her get it out," the Baby Doll said, crossing the courtyard and leaning against a big white column.

"Remember what I told you," the Bone Man said, ignoring the Baby Doll. "It ain't about the neighborhood. It's about the levees. How bad it got depends on how close you was to a levee break."

"Yeah, it was just a coincidence the levees broke where they did. It's just a coincidence people like us is homeless and them with dry houses don't look nothing like us," the Baby Doll said from across the courtyard.

Sister DeLille kneeled next to Trina. "Can she hear me?" she asked the Bone Man. Trina's brow was furrowed and her fists were clenched.

"It's not fair," she yelled before the Bone Man could answer. Suddenly the brightness of the day went gloomy, as if Trina had pulled a veil over the sky. The moment the darkness surrounded them, Sister DeLille swiveled away from Trina, clasped her hands tightly, and started to pray. The children stopped fidgeting and turned to stare at Trina.

"Are you breathing?" the Bone Man asked Trina. She took a few deep breaths, but her fists clenched tighter and the voices whirling around her body started to spark. The Bone Man stood and backed away. A soft crying sound rose up from among the children and water beaded on the surface of their skin.

"I gotta get Laveau over here," the Bone Man muttered to himself.

He stepped toward Sister DeLille, but she could not see or hear him. She had squeezed her eyes shut and pitched her voice louder to dig deeper into her prayers. He looked at the children, looked down Decatur toward the Marigny, then looked back at the children again. They were still wailing and leaking water that the Bone Man knew would collect at their feet and maybe even consume them all.

"They up there by the river," the Baby Doll said.

"What?"

"You looking for them, right? Big Chief, King Zulu, Flambeau. They went by the river."

The Bone Man gave the Baby Doll an appraising look.

"What you looking at me for?"

"I need you to watch them."

"Them?!? What the hell you think I can do about them? I ain't nothing but a…" She ran her hands through her ghostly flesh.

"I gotta get to Laveau. Quick. No telling what will happen if we can't stop this." An eerie whistling interrupted him. Both he and the Baby Doll looked over at Trina and the children. Trina had become catatonic and her skin was moist. The children were completely wet with water rolling down their bodies in tiny streams.

"I gotta go *now!*" the Bone Man yelled. "Make sure they don't flood out the Quarter before I get back."

Then he ran. He ran past the old U.S. Mint, through the crooked streets of the Marigny, past bars and restaurants in corner properties and brightly colored clapboard houses toward Louisa Street. His armpits became damp and his chest began to hurt as he stopped short around drunken celebrants and darted past crowds in the packed streets. Just as he was running over the train tracks, he saw a woman zip by on a bicycle wearing a purple poncho and a black-and-white patterned head wrap.

"Laveau!" the Bone Man screamed as she passed him. "Laveau!"

The woman squeezed the handbrakes and her bicycle came screeching to a halt. She looked back at the Bone Man and raised her eyebrows.

"I need your help," he said, gasping for breath.

"Does it have anything to do with that?" she asked, pointing to the sky.

In the distance, he could see a funnel of lightning rising up from the ground to part a thick patch of darkness that hovered in the sky.

The Bone Man nodded, "Yeah."

"Jump on," she said. "Talk while we ride."

With the wind blowing in his face, the Bone Man told Laveau everything—his confinement in the Lower 9th Ward, his discovery of the children, the second line, the children's bewildering powers, and their current state as tiny fountains throwing off sparks and tears. When he was done, Laveau was silent, steadily rising and dipping as she pedaled them forward.

"So what are they?" the Bone Man asked when she didn't speak. "Can you fix them?"

"I don't work like that," she said. "Won't know what to do until I see them."

The Bone Man said nothing more. He held on tight as Laveau pedaled up Decatur until she squeezed the brakes at Café du Monde and told him to hop off. She leaned her bike on a lamppost and grabbed the sack that was stuffed in her bike basket. She ran into the center of the courtyard and looked around.

"I thought you said you left them here," she said.

"I did," the Bone Man said.

The courtyard was empty. The Bone Man looked over to the column where the Baby Doll had been leaning. It was empty. Even Sister DeLille was nowhere to be seen. Then, from beyond the tree-lined courtyard, a flare of light erupted in the darkened sky.

"By the river!" the Bone Man yelled. He rushed out of the courtyard and to the nearby ramp that led to the river. He raced up the incline, Laveau hot on his heels. At the top, he paused and looked out toward the river. The children had found their way to a gravel-covered clearing. They stood in a circle with Trina in the center, electric flashes swirling around her body and funneling upward into the sky.

"See," he said, pointing to the layer of water pooling in the center of the circle.

Then he was off, speeding down the stairs before Laveau could say a word. At the bottom of the stairs, he saw that the children were not alone. The Big Chief, King Zulu, and the Flambeau were clustered near a short concrete wall in animated conversation. The Bone Man ran across the gravel, taking frequent glances up at the sky. The funnel of lightning was even more frightening from up close. When they reached the children, Laveau slung her bag across her chest and held her hands up, palms close to the children. He watched her walk in a slow circle around the children before leaving her to rush over to the men.

A string of dynamite—the same strand that had been around the Flambeau's neck—was lying on the ground at the men's feet.

"Dynamite!? That's why y'all disappeared?"

"That's why *he* disappeared," King Zulu said, jerking his head at the Flambeau.

"We came to stop him," the Big Chief added on.

"Somebody else made this town a fish bowl. Why shouldn't

all the fish get wet?" the Flambeau said. His expression looked petulant and unrepentant.

"So with all this suffering, you trying to bring another flood?" the Bone Man yelled.

"Just trying to even things out."

"You ain't God, fool!"

"I see you found Laveau," King Zulu said, silencing the Flambeau before he could speak again.

The men all turned to see Laveau continue to circle the children. While no one was looking, the Bone Man kicked the dynamite into the river.

"We don't need this shit," he said and ran back to Laveau.

When the Bone Man reached her side, Laveau stepped away from the children.

"They don't belong here," she said. The Bone Man inhaled a sharp breath. His gut clenched at the idea of sending them away.

"Where do you think they belong?" a voice said from behind the Bone Man and Leaveau.

They both turned to see Sister DeLille standing there, clutching her heavy silver cross. The lower half of her robes were wet where she had been kneeling to pray. Laveau nodded at her in greeting.

"Sister DeLille."

"She wanna know if you gonna send them to heaven or hell," the Baby Doll said, materializing next to Sister DeLille.

Laveau's eyes widened when she saw the Baby Doll appear out of thin air. Sister DeLille clutched tighter onto her cross and began a rapid fire whispering of holy chants.

"Oh, yes," said the Bone Man. "I forgot to tell you..."

Laveau nodded her head. "This is good," she said, cutting off the Bone Man. "I don't have the power to decide where they go from here. I can only make a pathway, but it will help if they have a guide." She switched her gaze to the Baby Doll.

"Who? Me?" the Baby Doll sputtered.

Laveau held her hands up as if to calm the Baby Doll.

"We all have a job to do. It's time for you to figure yours out."

The tightening of the Baby Doll's face was her only protest. Laveau—pretending not to notice the scowl on the Baby Doll's face—turned and ducked below the children's clasped hands to enter their circle. Wading through the water, she slipped her hands under her poncho and pulled out a dark-colored bar. She quickly ran her palms over the bar until her hands were coated and returned the bar to her pocket. Just as Trina's eyes had rolled back in her head, Laveau took a firm grasp of Trina's arms. The Bone Man, Sister DeLille, and the Baby Doll gasped. The Big Chief, King Zulu, and the Flambeau abandoned their arguing and crept closer, angling for a better view.

Trina stiffened, but the funnel of light fountaining up from her head did not cease. Laveau closed her eyes and cocked her head toward Trina as if listening. A low moan seeped from Laveau's lips. She shivered, then opened her eyes and let go of Trina. Everyone stared at her tense and expectant as she slowly waded back toward the ring of children and ducked beneath their clasped hands to exit their circle.

When her feet were no longer submerged in the water, she covered her face with her hands and started to cry. There was a moment of awkward silence as all the adults looked at her. Finally, Sister DeLille broke away from the group and placed a comforting arm around Laveau's shoulder.

"Are you okay?"

Laveau took a shaky breath and wiped her face.

"Only so much trauma a body can take," she said.

"Are they...?" Sister DeLille paused.

"What I gotta do?" the Baby Doll said, interrupting Sister DeLille.

Laveau shook her head, "It's not just you, I need everyone's help."

"You can't mean…" Sister DeLille said and traced this sign of the cross over her body.

"Yes," Laveau said.

Sister DeLille shook her head. "They are not human."

"They are not flesh," Laveau corrected her, "but they are ours. They are carrying our pain."

Sister DeLille's face tightened.

"I feel like I ain't flesh no more either," said the Flambeau.

Sister DeLille shook her head sharply.

"My prayer will be my help," she said and walked away from the group.

"You have my help," the Bone Man said, as Sister DeLille lowered herself to her knees. But Laveau did not hear him. She had wandered away to kick at the gravel and search for stones.

"What is she doing?" the Flambeau asked.

"We're not the ones to ask," King Zulu said.

The Bone Man glanced up to the sky and he froze, his heart seizing with fright.

"No, no, no," he yelled as he rushed over to Laveau. He yanked at her arm and gestured wildly to the sky. "You have to do something quick or they will take the children."

Laveau glanced up. The sky was filling up with those floating patches of water—rows and rows of them hovering overhead and swooping overhead.

"They can't get any closer," she said. "That one," she said and paused to point her chin at Trina, "is keeping them away." She calmly returned to her task of searching the gravel. "Make yourself useful," she said. "Hold these."

She placed a collection of black stones in the Bone Man's outstretched palms. While she leaned over to place the rocks in a complicated pattern on the ground, the Bone Man looked into the sky again. Laveau was right. The patches of water were bobbing in the air, dripping from their edges, but they drifted no closer. When Laveau's pattern was complete, it stretched all the way around the children, enclosing them in a ring of stone. Laveau stood and brushed the dirt off her hands.

"We ready?" she asked.

Sister DeLille kept praying, the Bone Man nodded, and the Baby Doll disappeared.

"We need some music," she yelled.

"Don't we need her," the Bone Man whispered, pointing to the spot where the Baby Doll had been standing.

"Don't worry," Laveau said. "Everyone will do their job." She spoke with a steeliness that did not invite dissent.

On that cue, the Big Chief lifted his tambourine and rattled it fiercely. The vibrating sound ran through everyone like an electric current. He threw his head back and started to chant. Without hesitation, the Flambeau joined in, lifting and dropping his pole so that it struck the ground in syncopation with the Big Chief's chant. King Zulu added to the rhythm with polyrhythmic handclaps. Laveau opened her arms and swayed to the beat of the three men's song. Her lips were moving in their own prayer, calling for support, pleading for guidance, asking that the children be led home. Then she re-entered the children's circle.

The Bone Man sang softly while shifting his view between Laveau and the patches of water floating in the sky. Laveau stood next to a child and raised her hands. She threw a loud stream of words into the sky and in response one of the patches of water began to drift down toward them. The Bone Man sprinted forward, racing to reach the child first. He tried to duck under the children's clasped hands and enter the circle, but he was shoved backward by some unseen force. He paced around the circle, impotent, as the patch of water swooped low and hovered over Laveau and the child. Laveau lowered her head and firmed her stance. In the shadow of the water, the Baby Doll materialized again. The Bone Man hunched down to watch.

Without a word, the Baby Doll swept the child into a tight embrace. Surrounded by the Baby Doll's limbs, the child sighed before being completely overtaken by trembling. The Baby Doll held on more tightly as a ghostly form rose up from the crown of the child's head, floated upward, and slipped into the rippling patch of water overhead. The child fell backward, dragging the Baby Doll with her. They both splashed into the water that had collected in the circle.

When he saw that the Baby Doll dissolved, the second she made contact with the water, the Bone Man rose up to his hands and knees. He gritted his teeth and scrambled forward, ducking into the children's circle with as much force as he could muster. The invisible barrier contracted softly, then popped and the Bone Man went tumbling into the circle. Struggling forward, he fought the pull of the water to reach the child. Leaning over, he reached down to lift her from the water. Stunned to find that she was solid—not ghostly—under his touch, he scooped her up and carried her, soaking wet and shivering, over to Sister DeLille.

"It worked," he said, rousing the sister from her prayers.

"What worked?"

"They are whole again!" said the Bone Man. "Do you really have space for them?"

Sister DeLille reached out tentatively. Her hand shook as she stroked the child's shoulder. When she saw the girl was flesh and bone, she grabbed the child close and dried her off as best she could with her robes.

"It's a true miracle," she said, but the Bone Man did not hear her. He had already rushed back to the circle just as two patches of water were absorbing the ghostly forms of two more children. When the Bone Man reached them, they were giggling and splashing each other with water. He grabbed their hands and ushered them away out of the circle. He handed them over to Sister DeLille with tears in his eyes. These were not the heavy tears that had clogged his throat since the storm. These were tears of hope. They streamed down his cheeks, gifting him with the sweet release of relief. Each time he rushed back to the circle and returned to Sister DeLille with the newly freed children, his spirit felt lighter.

No matter how many times he had to go and return, the Bone Man did not falter. In fact, not one of them lost the rhythm of their work. Laveau was unwavering as she freed child after child. The Baby Doll was tireless as a guide, as she reappeared again and again, no matter how many times she was doused in the water. The Big Chief, King Zulu, and the Flambeau were unflagging as they provided potent sonic strength that fueled the children's return to flesh.

After the last child had been released, Laveau finally turned to chant over Trina. Trina's neck was craned back as if she were staring up at the last patch of water left hovering in the sky. The lightning shooting from Trina's body plunged into the patch of water creating, a stream of steam that tumbled over everyone's heads. The Baby Doll materialized behind Trina and wrapped her arms around Trina's shoulders. Laveau joined the embrace, circling her arms around Trina and the Baby Doll both. Desperate to keep Trina safe, the Bone Man pressed into the crush of bodies, wrapping his arms around all three of them. Suddenly Laveau stiffened. She made a deep guttural sound in her throat and jerked her head one, two, three times. Trina seemed to collapse into herself as her head lolled onto Laveau's arm and her body fell slack.

Another wave of tears rushed through the Bone Man as he knelt, reaching past the Baby Doll and Laveau's legs to scoop Trina up. He didn't see the Baby Doll go crashing into the water one last time. He didn't hear the strain in the men's voices as they pushed through hoarseness to keep the song going. All he was aware of was the weight of Trina's body as he crushed her against his chest. He held onto Trina tightly as it all washed over him: all he had lost, all the city had suffered, all he knew he would continue to endure. For a few brief seconds, the mania and grief that had been holding him hostage loosened. With Trina in his arms, he waded through the water, calming his impulse to run, to surge forward and fly her somewhere safe so that when she woke he could tell her with a smile what she was, tell her that there would be no more drifting and no more ghostliness, let her know that her mind and spirit could rest because he would take care of her, because she was once again flesh and blood, and they had made it to the other side—that, together, they were finally home.

ACKNOWLEDGEMENTS

"There is a vitality, a life-force, an energy, a quickening that is translated through you into action, and because there is only one of you in all time, this expression is unique. And if you block it, it will never exist through any other medium and will be lost." — Martha Graham

I am grateful to the confluence of events and people that have carried me forward and supported me as I continue working at adding my creative voice to the great ocean of human expression.

GROWTH: I'm thankful for growth that allows me to put my head down and create as the business of life continues whizzing by me.

ROOTS: Grateful to my parents Tayari and Kalamu Salaam who have supported my writing with enthusiasm and confidence; and to my father for suggesting that I publish my first story. That first publication~which came with a $100 check~had everything to do with me believing I was a writer from the beginning.

AMPLIFICATION: Thank you to L. Timmel Duchamp and Aqueduct for publishing my first collection, and to the Tiptree Award committee for recognizing its merit and worth. Thank you, Tayari Jones, for sharing the opportunities that come across your desk and connecting me with Third Man Books. Thank you to Third Man Books for seeking work that's outside the box.

SUPPORT: Thank you to Sheree Renée Thomas for her generous editorial eye, Kris Dikeman for her copy review, and my two long-term readers: my brother Mtume Salaam and my friend Mary Lou Johnson who always offer their unvarnished opinion of my work.

COLLEAGUES: To the many writing communities I am a part of~Altered Fluid, Sycamore Hill, Clarion West class of 2001, the New York writers who disrupt assumptions of what a sci-fi/spec-fic writer is~thank you for your presence, support, critique, and example. I love to receive word of your successes and to learn from your challenges.

CREW: I'd be nowhere without my beloved crews that hold me together and keep me sane. Currently that includes my writing partner Lynn Pitts; my family crew of my sisters Asante and Tiaji Salaam and my cousins Maisha and Kina Joshua; and my NYC fam (who have all abandoned me) Zenobia Connor, Kenya Miles, Nneka Bennett, and Jenga Mwendo; and my "co-parent" Iliana Quander.

"The Taming" originally appeared in *Interfictions Online: A Journal of Interstitial Arts*, Issue 6, November 2015. It has been newly edited for this collection.

ABOUT THE AUTHOR

Kiini Ibura Salaam is a writer, painter, and traveler from New Orleans, Louisiana. Her work is rooted in eroticism, speculative events, and personal freedom. She has been widely published and anthologized in such publications as the *Dark Matter, Mojo: Conjure Stories,* and *Colonize This!* anthologies, as well as *Essence, Utne Reader,* and *Ms.* magazines. Her short story collection *Ancient, Ancient*—winner of the 2012 James Tiptree, Jr. award—contains sensual tales of the fantastic, the dark, and the magical. Her microessays on writing can be found at www.kiiniibura.com or in her *Notes From the Trenches* ebook series. *When the World Wounds* is her second collection of speculative short stories.